A DEADLY HAND

MACON FALLON HAD never felt more calm, more ready. "You tried to cheat me, Graham, but you're small-time. You aren't really good with cards. On the river they would laugh at you.

"Now I am going to give you a chance. I am going to give you ten minutes to get out of town!"

Graham was trembling with hatred and bitterness. He was going to kill Fallon. He was going to shoot him in the guts and let him die slow.

Graham reached for his hat with his left hand. His right hand disappeared behind the hat, and then Macon Fallon drew. . . .

Bantam Books by Louis L'Amour

NOVELS
Bendigo Shafter
Borden Chantry
Brionne
The Broken Gun
The Burning Hills
The Californios
Callaghen
Catlow
Chancy
The Cherokee Trail
Comstock Lode
Conagher
Crossfire Trail
Dark Canyon
Down the Long Hills
The Empty Land
Fair Blows the Wind
Fallon
The Ferguson Rifle
The First Fast Draw
Flint
Guns of the Timberlands
Hanging Woman Creek
The Haunted Mesa
Heller with a Gun
The High Graders
High Lonesome
Hondo
How the West Was Won
The Iron Marshal
The Key-Lock Man
Kid Rodelo
Kilkenny
Killoe
Kilrone
Kiowa Trail
Last of the Breed
Last Stand at Papago Wells
The Lonesome Gods
The Man Called Noon
The Man from Skibbereen
The Man from
    the Broken Hills
Matagorda
Milo Talon
The Mountain Valley War
North to the Rails
Over on the Dry Side
Passin' Through
The Proving Trail

The Quick and the Dead
Radigan
Reilly's Luck
The Rider of Lost Creek
Rivers West
The Shadow Riders
Shalako
Showdown at
    Yellow Butte
Silver Canyon
Sitka
Son of a Wanted Man
Taggart
The Tall Stranger
To Tame a Land
Tucker
Under the
    Sweetwater Rim
Utah Blaine
The Walking Drum
Westward the Tide
Where the Long Grass
    Blows

SHORT STORY COLLECTIONS
Beyond the Great
    Snow Mountains
Bowdrie
Bowdrie's Law
Buckskin Run
The Collected Short
    Stories of Louis
    L'Amour (vols. 1–7)
Dutchman's Flat
End of the Drive
From the Listening Hills
The Hills of Homicide
Law of the Desert Born
Long Ride Home
Lonigan
May There Be a Road
Monument Rock
Night Over the Solomons
Off the Mangrove Coast
The Outlaws of Mesquite
The Rider of
    the Ruby Hills
Riding for the Brand
The Strong Shall Live
The Trail to Crazy Man
Valley of the Sun

War Party
West from Singapore
West of Dodge
With These Hands
Yondering

SACKETT TITLES
Sackett's Land
To the Far Blue Mountains
The Warrior's Path
Jubal Sackett
Ride the River
The Daybreakers
Sackett
Lando
Mojave Crossing
Mustang Man
The Lonely Men
Galloway
Treasure Mountain
Lonely on the Mountain
Ride the Dark Trail
The Sackett Brand
The Sky-Liners

**THE HOPALONG
    CASSIDY NOVELS**
The Riders of High Rock
The Rustlers of West Fork
The Trail to Seven Pines
Trouble Shooter

NONFICTION
Education of a
    Wandering Man
Frontier
The Sackett Companion:
    A Personal Guide to
    the Sackett Novels
A Trail of Memories:
    The Quotations of
    Louis L'Amour,
    compiled by
    Angelique L'Amour

POETRY
Smoke from This Altar

LOST TREASURES
Louis L'Amour's Lost
    Treasures: Volume 1
No Traveller Returns

FALLON

A NOVEL

Louis L'Amour

Postscript by Beau L'Amour

BANTAM BOOKS
NEW YORK

Fallon is a work of fiction. Names, characters, places,
and incidents are the products of the author's imagination or
are used fictitiously. Any resemblance to actual events, locales,
or persons, living or dead, is entirely coincidental.

2019 Bantam Books Mass Market Edition

Copyright © 1963 by Louis & Katherine L'Amour Trust
Postscript by Beau L'Amour copyright © 2019 by Beau L'Amour

Published in the United States by Bantam Books, an imprint of
Random House, a division of Penguin Random House LLC, New York.

BANTAM and the HOUSE colophon are registered trademarks of
Penguin Random House LLC.

Originally published in paperback in the United States
by Bantam Books, an imprint of Random House, a division of
Penguin Random House LLC, in 1970.

ISBN 978-0-593-12990-6
Ebook ISBN 978-0-593-12991-3

Cover art: Gregory Manchess

Printed in the United States of America

randomhousebooks.com

2 4 6 8 9 7 5 3 1

Bantam Books mass market edition: May 2019

To
WINDY SLIM:
Who Knew Every Side-Track West
of the Mississippi

FALLON

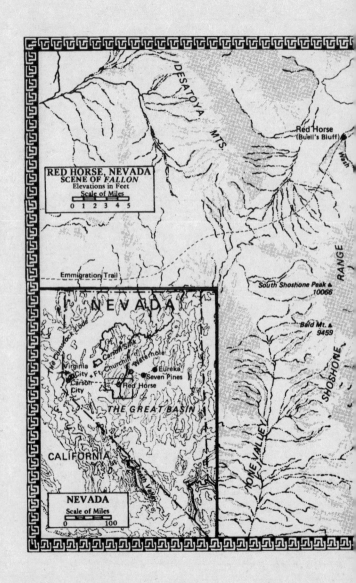

RED HORSE, NEVADA
SCENE OF *FALLON*
Elevations in Feet
Scale of Miles
0 1 2 3 4 5

DESATOYA MTS

Red Horse
(Buell's Bluff)

Wash

South Shoshone Peak
10066

Bald Mt.
9459

SHOSHONE RANGE

Emmigration Trail

NEVADA

The Comstock Lode

Virginia City

Carson City

Carson Sink

Churchill Ft.

Waterhole

Eureka

Seven Pines

Red Horse

THE GREAT BASIN

CALIFORNIA

Death Valley

ONE VALLEY

NEVADA
Scale of Miles
0   100

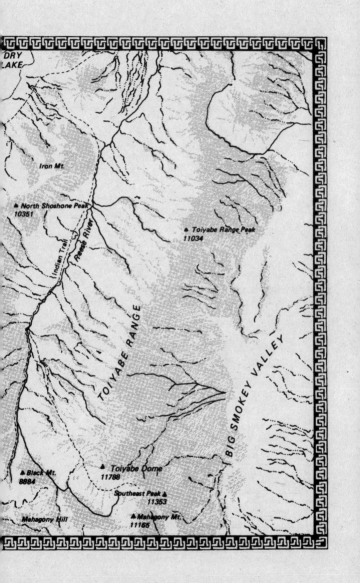

CHAPTER 1

MACON FALLON WAS a stranger to the town of Seven Pines, and fortunately for him he was a stranger with a fast horse.

In the course of an eventful life, Macon Fallon had become a connoisseur of western hospitality, and knew when a limit had been reached.

Hence, when an escorting party, complete with rope, arranged to conduct him to the vicinity of a large cottonwood where the evening's festivities would be concluded, he wasted no time on formalities, but promptly departed the premises.

The moment chosen was, of course, appropriate to the situation. The self-appointed posse were as confident as a few drinks could make them, but were totally unaware of the quality of the man they escorted.

One of the riders had lagged a little, and at that moment they came abreast of an opening in the brush that walled the trail. Fallon rode an excellent cutting horse that could turn on a dime.

The black horse went through the opening with a bound and, sensing the urgency of its rider, took off on a dead run.

No horse Fallon had ever seen could catch that black

of his in under half a mile, and by the time that distance lay behind, Fallon was prepared to resort to evasive tactics. The black had staying quality as well as an initial burst of speed; and the posse, less superbly mounted, fell rapidly behind.

Unfortunately, by the time the opportunity for escape was offered, only one direction remained to Fallon . . . and westward lay a waterless waste . . . or one that was relatively so.

The nearest water hole was thirty miles off, but on Fallon's one previous visit the water there had been plentiful and good. With a safe lead, and some tracks purposely left to indicate that he had circled the town, he settled down for a long ride.

At thirty miles, with his throat parched for a drink, the water hole proved to be a bed of dried, cracked mud.

At forty-two miles, with his horse stumbling, the creek was a dusty trough, and Macon Fallon was a man in trouble.

Somewhere behind was a posse of irate citizens who had by this time found his trail. They would be coming along with filled canteens and could afford to ignore the water holes.

To the best of his knowledge, which admittedly was not thorough, the next seventy miles offered no water.

Dust sifted over him, and sweat etched a fine pattern of lines upon his lean, ruggedly handsome if somewhat saturnine features. He dismounted, talked to the horse to reassure it, then walked on, leading the horse.

He was a man naturally considerate of horses, but he also knew that in this country if his horse should die, his own death was only a matter of time.

———

THE TROUBLE IN Seven Pines had been none of his own making. It has been written that while Man proposes, God disposes; but when Macon Fallon joined that poker game he had no idea he was sitting in on an invitation to death.

He had money, a good horse, and time for a leisurely ride south. The poker game was merely a means to endure a dull evening in a strange town; whether he won or lost was unimportant.

His mood was pleasant, his prospects excellent, and the future looked good indeed, yet when he drew back that chair at the poker table, he sat down to trouble.

The game began innocently enough. He won a small pot, lost two. . . . As the evening progressed he drew no very interesting cards. By midnight he was winner to the tune of six silver dollars, and was ready to turn in. At that moment, destiny took a hand.

Now, Fallon was a man who could do things with cards. He could, while shuffling, run up a top stock or a bottom stock; he could shift the cut, deal from the top or the bottom, or second-deal; and he knew all about slick aces, marked or trimmed cards, shiners, mirrors in pipebowls or match boxes, and the tiny pricks on finger rings for the purpose of marking cards.

Sleeve and belt holdouts were no mystery to him, and he knew all about the man who brings drinks or sandwiches to the table with a cold deck held underneath the tray ready for a switch. In short, Macon Fallon was a professional; and although usually honest, he was not above cheating the cheaters if they invited it.

On this night he was playing a fair game, and was not especially interested in winning.

Suddenly he was dealt an ace, another ace, and a third one. He discarded two indifferent cards, and was rewarded with two queens. The pot was very satisfactory, and no comment was made.

The following hand he received two sevens and a pair of jacks, then drew a third seven. Once more the pot was a pleasant one; and a player named Collins, a popular man locally, gave him a long, careful look and commented, "You are lucky tonight."

"I think I'll turn in," Fallon said, stifling a yawn. "I've a long ride tomorrow."

Collins glanced at him. "You have a good deal of our money. Better give us a chance to win it back."

"Two more hands then," Fallon agreed. "I'm dead tired."

Instinct warned that he should get out while the getting was good, but even as he spoke the deal was progressing. It was with relief that he picked up two fours. He would lose this hand, then he would quit.

He contributed liberally to the pot, and on the draw he picked up the other two fours.

Four of a kind . . .

Recognizing his dismay, they misunderstood its reason. Promptly, they began to raise, and Macon Fallon was not a man to look gift horses in the teeth, nor will any gambler in his right mind betray his luck.

Besides, there was a poem he recalled, a poem that went something like this:

If he play, being young and unskillful,
For shekels of silver and gold—

Take his money, my son, praising Allah,
*The kid was ordained to be sold.**

Unfortunately, that drawing of fours was followed by the drawing of sixes, and Collins lost on that draw also. He started to take action, and Fallon, forced to deal, placed two aces of lead, neatly spaced over the heart of Collins, where they might have been covered by a blue chip.

The shooting was fair, and nobody had seen anything wrong with the play, but Collins had been a popular man and nobody wanted to see all that money leave Seven Pines.

A self-appointed committee convened and it was decided to hang Fallon, whereupon the committee repaired to the bar to drink to their decision. Several drinks later Macon Fallon was led to his horse and started along the road toward the selected cottonwood.

Befuddled by too many toasts to the occasion, and exhilarated by the prospect of excitement in town, they neglected to search Fallon's saddlebags or even to remove the rifle from its scabbard. After all, his hands were bound behind him and they had only half a mile to go.

It could not be said that Macon Fallon was a man who missed opportunities, or was laggard in putting time to use. No sooner was he seated in the saddle than he began straining his fingers to reach the knots that bound his wrists, a proceeding considerably facilitated by the fact that he had taken the precaution of tensing his muscles as they bound him, which permitted a little slack.

He had, on a couple of previous occasions, been witness to hangings, and the proceedings had filled him with

---

* Certain Maxims of Hafiz, by Rudyard Kipling.

distaste. The prospect of being the central figure in such a ceremony attracted him not at all.

Yet dying of thirst was scarcely preferable, and that appeared to be the alternative he had chosen. Walking and riding with these thoughts in his mind, Fallon covered ten miles more.

He was now devoid of any illusions as to the outcome. He simply was not going to make it, and neither was his horse. The blazing sun had taken its toll, as had the stifling dust.

He might have tried to seek out shade and wait for the cooler hours, but the posse was somewhere behind him and they would not lack for water.

Fallon remounted, and the black horse started gamely on. They would be fortunate to last another three miles.

At that moment he saw the wagons. They were no mirage.

Two covered wagons, two teams of six oxen each, two saddle horses, a milk cow, and half a dozen people. One wagon was canted sharply over, a condition he diagnosed as a broken wheel. Oxen and horses were gaunt, the people drawn and tired.

Hastily, in the moment before they sighted him, Fallon beat the dust from his clothing, straightened his tie, pulled his horse's head up, and straightened up himself. He would approach them as a man of means, a man of spirit, a man who could take command. Once people felt pity for a man, he would never be able to have the upper hand. The thing to do was take command and keep them moving.

Macon Fallon was alive to opportunity, and opportunity was what he needed now. Every bit of his cash except for a few dollars had been left behind in Seven Pines.

He needed not only a stake before going on, but a chance for his horse and himself to recover strength.

And these were the people who would provide it. Did not the good Lord send the lambs to be sheared?

Macon Fallon was a cynic, but every cynic is a sentimentalist under the skin, and therein lay the chink in Fallon's armor of larceny. For basically, no matter how much he might consider himself otherwise, Macon Fallon was a gentleman in the best sense of the word.

Aware of his deficiency, he avoided every contact that might betray him into thoughtfulness, gallantry, or consideration. He kept to himself, and when necessity demanded that he deal harshly, he ruthlessly dealt so with those who were themselves so inclined.

People, he told himself, were suckers. The fact that on several occasions he had proved to be one himself only served to illustrate the point.

Two assets belonged to Fallon besides a glib tongue and a gift for handling the pasteboards. One was a keen sense of observation; the other, an excellent memory and a mind filled to overflowing with an enormous variety of usually useless information.

Long ago he had discovered that while all people look, there are few who actually *see*. Rarely did people look with intelligence, or recognize what they were seeing. If they walked in the forest they saw only trees; or at best, merely certain varieties of trees.

But Macon Fallon saw much more. He saw where a bear had stood on his hind legs and had left his mark to other bears as high as he could reach upon the trunk; he saw where a deer had passed, and how long since; where blight had touched a tree, or where lightning had scarred one long ago. He saw these things, and much, much more.

So, when he glimpsed the wagons his mind was not so gripped by the sight of them that he failed to see lying in the brush, almost obliterated by the weather, a faded sign: BUELL'S BLUFF.

Buell's Bluff?

Startled, he drew up and looked again and immediately the sign, the people of the wagons, and his own fertile imagination became the base upon which he began to construct a plan. His thoughts leaped ahead. If the plan worked he could, in a few weeks, at most in a few months, ride into California completely solvent.

He drew himself still straighter in the saddle, cocked his hat at a still jauntier angle, and attempted to look as spruce as he did not feel. The lambs awaited, and he held the shears. A question remained: did the lambs have fleece?

His lethargy was gone, his weariness fell away, even the heat and his own parched throat and cracked lips were forgotten; for here was opportunity, and no man had ever needed one more.

Even as he advanced, he could not but wonder if he did not look like a dusty Don Quixote . . . if so, the black horse was, at least, no Rosinante. Undoubtedly he was in worse shape than they, but he had probably had more experience with adversity than they could possibly have had.

There were two men, two women of mature years, a boy of sixteen, two young girls, and three smaller children. There was also a young man of perhaps nineteen.

Sweeping off his hat as only he knew how, Fallon asked, "May I be of service?"

"Wheel broke." The speaker was a man of about forty-five, with sandy hair, a well-shaped head, and a strong face. "We got the know-how, but we ain't got the tools."

Macon Fallon stepped carefully from the saddle, trying not to stagger. With that bulging water-sack hanging from the side of the wagon, with that smell of bacon frying, absolutely nothing was going to get him away from here. Yet he must seem prosperous; anything else at this time would prove fatal to his plan.

"You are going to the mines?"

The worry in the sandy-haired man's face was apparent. "Small chance unless we leave our wagons and start off afoot." He indicated the shimmering wasteland. "We're kind of scared to tackle that, with the womenfolks, and all."

Salvation lay here for Fallon, not only for the moment, but for the future as well, if he could play these people in the right way. His throat was raw with the need for water, and the smell of food made his stomach growl with impatience.

"Rightly so." He gestured toward the barren country around them. "A man without a horse out there, and without water . . . he *might* keep going two days if he was strong to begin with."

Fallon's glance fell on one of the girls . . . quickly he averted his eyes. This was no time for sentiment.

These were good people, the sort he usually avoided, but he could not think of that now. In any event, it was not them he planned to victimize. They would be merely the window dressing.

And anyway, what else could they do? Where could they go? With luck, the men might make it through; the women and children never could.

Fallon opened his campaign with a wide, friendly smile.

"Believe me, you are more fortunate than you realize. That wheel of yours must have been inspired to break down here. You need go no farther."

He turned to the water barrel. "May I?"

Dipping water into his hat with the drinking gourd, he held it for his grateful horse. He took only the smallest sip himself, but it sent an agonizing, unbelievable coolness throughout his body.

When his horse had emptied the hat, Fallon hung up the gourd. His eyes at that moment fell upon the sorrel horse tied to the tailgate of the other wagon, and he seemed to consider for a moment. "Have you ever heard," he asked, "of the town of Red Horse?"

He moved closer to the fire and the bacon, fighting the urge to drink more, and still more. "Red Horse," he continued, "was a mining town born suddenly from a rocky gorge. It was said to be the richest strike among the mines."

He paused . . . would nobody offer him a cup of coffee?

"My Uncle Joe, God rest his soul, was among the founders, owner of the richest claim. Then the Piutes came . . . suddenly in the night . . . and every man-jack of them was slaughtered . . . wiped out."

He glanced around the group, then moved again to the water barrel and dipped the gourd. All eyes were upon him, all were listening avidly, except one girl, who looked at him with cool, disdainful eyes.

He touched the gourd to his lips and allowed a little more water to trickle to the parched tissues of his mouth and throat.

"The town and the claims were forgotten. They had existed too short a time to be generally known, those who knew the most about the place were dead, the claims were deserted, the buildings empty."

He sipped water again. "One thing, and one only, prevented Red Horse from being forever lost."

He had their attention, all right. They had forgotten their troubles, even forgotten where they were, yet he knew it was less what he said that was important than what their imaginations would do to the story.

"My uncle," he said, "had written a letter." He put his hand on his breast. "I have it . . . here."

"That's all very well, mister." It was the girl with the skeptical eyes. "But what has that to do with us?"

Fallon held a mouthful of water for an instant before swallowing it. And he knew his horse would be desperate for more, having had not more than a few swallows.

"Do I smell coffee? And bacon?" No use waiting for an invitation. "Perhaps we could discuss the situation over supper?"

His strategy had only begun, and he needed time. He had his overall plan, but there were ramifications to be worked out.

He had already decided that these were no lambs ready for the fleecing, for they had little—at least, by his standards. A few supplies, some equipment, their weapons, the animals and wagons. He doubted they had cash to any amount; but one of the wagons had several packing cases that he could see.

The younger ones still clung, no doubt, to a dream of golden riches from the mines. The older ones—he knew the signs—had long since begun to disbelieve. The present disaster had been the clincher, and now they were frightened. Hardship they understood and could take;

struggle, poverty—these were expected. But now they feared death, and riches they no longer hoped for.

With the eyes of one who had often looked upon men in trouble, he knew that these people had come to the end of their resources.

Heat, dust, exhaustion, and the seemingly limitless miles that lay ahead had robbed them of their strength. They no longer knew which way to turn. Their stock was weak from hunger, the water in the barrels was stale, and it was insufficient for the trip that lay before them.

And besides all that, what they now lacked was hope, and that he meant to give them. In Buell's Bluff there could be no hope, so he had invented Red Horse.

What's in a name? A town by any other name can be as big a fraud.

Yes, he could give them hope, but he was honest enough to attribute no motives to himself that he did not deserve. The truth was, he needed these people for his own purposes. What he had in mind was a colossal swindle, but if he brought it off he could then proceed to San Francisco in style.

As he talked, he became eloquent. They could go on if they so desired. The trail lay open before them. It was true their stock looked bad, and their wagons were overloaded for what lay ahead. It was, he went on, at least fifty miles to the next water—he saw what a shock that gave them—but if what they wanted was land, gold, or a business of their own, they need go no farther.

As he talked, he ate. He drank coffee, he ate again.

And as he talked he found himself putting ideas into words that he had not even dreamed of before. Possibilities occurred to him as he spoke.

From an inner pocket he drew an envelope, and on the back of the letter he drew up an agreement.

"The town of Red Horse," he said, "belongs to me, but it has been abandoned for years. It occupies an intermediate point upon the trail, and with the coming of spring there will be money to be made.

"People will arrive here as you have arrived. They will be short of provisions, almost out of water, and they will need to lay in supplies. For this they will be ready to exchange goods or pay cash.

"I have here an agreement. Those who wish to go no farther, and wish to come with me to Red Horse, will sign it. Those who sign will move to Red Horse with me. We will brush up and clean up, and open the town for business. You may sort out whatever you can spare and put it up for sale."

"I brought a stock of goods," one man said suddenly. "Planned to keep store in California."

"Good! We will sell them at—" He caught himself just in time, for he had started to say 'at exorbitant prices,' but hastily dropped the adjective. Macon Fallon had observed that even merchants who sell at exorbitant prices do not like to admit to it.

"You will be free to stake claims as long as you leave mine alone, but let me assure you the finding of gold in paying quantity, either here or in California, is a very rare thing. The real gold will lie in the pockets of those who come to hunt for gold.

"Whether they find gold or not, they must eat, wear clothing, use tools. I will take thirty percent of your business profits, ten percent of your claims."

"That's ridiculous!" It was that girl with the cool eyes who spoke. "We provide the goods, and you take thirty percent! Why, we can go farther west, set up shop, and keep it all!"

He smiled at her across the heads of the others, admiring her slender figure, the way she stood straight on her two feet. At the same time, he wished she were already in California—or back where she came from. Anywhere but here, now.

"The way west is open, of course," he said. "You don't need me."

He turned abruptly and walked back to his horse, filling his hat again from the barrel. He was not worried, for he knew what they must do.

After giving his horse water, he occupied the next few minutes in brushing the dust from his coat, and wiping the action of his Winchester.

His wrists were still raw from the chafing of the rope, and he had to watch to keep his cuffs over the marks.

From his saddlebags he took his spare .44 and holstered it. It was his good fortune that the lynching party had been both drunk and overconfident.

As he brushed himself off and checked his guns, he considered the situation. Until he glimpsed that weathered sign lying forgotten in the brush, he had not thought of Buell's Bluff in years. Never having seen a map of the area, and approaching it from a different direction, he had not even realized he was in the vicinity. He had been one of those who had followed that ill-fated gold rush so long ago. Of course, the town might have burned, but he thought not. At least something would be left. And as he recalled, there was water on the site.

The niche in the hills where the town lay was well hidden, and there was small chance it had been rediscovered, or that any of the original miners had returned.

Buell's Bluff had been in the beginning what he was about to make it again—a fraud and a deception.

Yet, he told himself, how could these people do better? At least it would give their stock a chance to rest and recuperate.

With their overloaded wagons they could never cross the desert to the west. Their oxen were already tried beyond their endurance. One or two would surely die, then the others would be unable to haul the wagons, and then more would die.

These were good people, and he planned no deception for them—at least, not one that would cost them anything. And he did offer them hope, and some security without going farther.

He could hear them arguing, and the girl protesting. Why couldn't she keep her pretty mouth shut?

After several minutes the sandy-haired man walked over to him and thrust out his hand. "My name is Blane. This is Tom Damon. Is there gold there? At Red Horse?"

He had them now.

"My uncle said it was the richest strike in the mines." The most gold his uncle had ever seen was in his wife's wedding ring. "Naturally, I can promise nothing. I do not know what there is."

He paused. "Remember this: we do not have to find gold to do business. There will be trade with the wagon trains."

Blane scowled. "There will be a saloon. I do not hold with whiskey-drinking."

"Leave that to me. There will be order in the town."

"All right," Blane agreed finally. "It is a hard bargain you drive, but we have no choice."

Would the trail be washed out? Fallon knew what

heavy rains could do to any trail in this country; so at his suggestion all the oxen were hitched to one wagon, leaving young Jim Blane, who was sixteen, and Al Damon, who was nineteen, to guard the remaining wagon. Once arrived in Red Horse, they could dismount a wheel and return for the other wagon.

Macon Fallon, somewhat shamed by the hope he now saw in their faces, rode ahead to guide them. He had gone only a short distance when Ginia Blane overtook him.

Ginia obviously was not one to beat about the chaparral. "Mr. Fallon," she said, "is this a wild-goose chase?"

Something warned Macon Fallon that lying to Ginia would not be easy. The direct look from those cool gray eyes was disconcerting.

Buell's Bluff, hastily rechristened Red Horse, had been a monumental fraud, a gold rush promoted with a few carefully salted claims. Before the fraud was discovered men had rushed in, built stores, saloons, and a hotel. Investors who had missed the Comstock rushed to hand their money to the swindlers of Buell's Bluff.

Then a salted mine was found, others were hastily investigated, and within hours the exodus had begun. Within days the town was deserted. When the bottom fell out, the thud with which it fell was felt as far away as Boston, New York, and even London.

That had been ten years ago, and so far as Fallon was aware, nobody had been near the place since.

"Gold," he declared with great originality, "is where you find it—and one never knows. It was *said* to be a great strike, but after the Piute attack it was deserted."

That statement was true. It had been *said* to be a great

strike, and Piutes had killed the last men to leave the town. Nine men had died in that sudden raid.

"I don't trust you, Mr. Fallon," Ginia said, "and if you take advantage of us I shall find a way to make you pay."

No tracks showed on the trail, nor any evidence of travel. Heavy rains had gouged gullies across the road, and in places had turned the trail itself into a water-course, cutting deep ruts. Fallon stopped several times to roll rocks into the deeper ruts, or to kick down the sides and make passage easier for the wagon.

The town lay upon a long bench that bordered a wash on the far side. Actually, the wash curved around the bench, which was more than a mile long. The town was backed up against the mountain at the farthest end of the bench, and behind the town there was a scattering of trees. Altogether, as he recalled it, the site was far from uninviting.

Yet nothing in the country over which they rode suggested any town, or any evidence of water. It was singularly barren and depressing.

Suddenly Ginia Blane drew rein. "Where are you taking us? It's been miles, and there's simply nothing."

"If I recall," he replied mildly, "you will see the town from the top of that rise."

Suspicious, but willing to give him a chance to prove his case, she rode on with him. They topped out suddenly on the hill overlooking the valley, and the town lay before them, about a mile away. At this distance, it seemed that time had not produced any visible change.

It was even larger than he recalled, for there was a street with at least a dozen business buildings, and a scattering of houses and shacks. In sudden panic he tried to remember whether any of the signs carried the name of Buell's Bluff.

He turned to Ginia. "You had best ride back to the wagons. They might not realize the town is so near and decide to camp for the night. They should come on through."

Her eyes searched his face. "Is that the only reason you want me to go back?"

She was lovely, no question of that. She had an attractive figure and a charming face; but she was his enemy, suspicious of his every word and move.

"Actually," he replied, "it is not my only reason. So far as I know the town is deserted, but I cannot be sure. When I ride in I wish to be alone, responsible only for myself."

"Also"—this was a sudden inspiration—"in a town so long abandoned there are sure to be snakes. This country is infested with rattlers."

He had scored a point, for she drew up instantly, but she was still suspicious. "You find explanations very easy, don't you, Mr. Fallon? You are very glib, very smooth. You are also," she added, "quite a handsome man, very rugged-looking and strong, but I think you are a sham, Mr. Fallon."

Deliberately, she turned her horse and rode back to the wagons, and he looked after her, feeling no resentment.

Before him lay the town. The sun was setting beyond the distant ridges and they carried a crimson glow along their serrated edges. He cantered down the hill, thinking of the water that lay ahead, as the black horse undoubtedly was also.

Never far behind any boom, Macon Fallon had followed the will-o'-the-wisp of fortune to this place, too, only he was younger then, and fortune seemed much closer.

Yet now, if all went well, he might accomplish his objective and sell out within ninety days. It was doubtful if anyone in this land of shifting population would remember the place. People never stopped in this area, but passed on through, bound for California.

His horse's hoofs drummed on the old plank bridge, still sturdy and solid. Sleeping echoes awakened, warning anyone who might be holed up within the town.

Slowing to a walk, he drew his Winchester. At the near end of the street he drew up, studying the situation.

The windows stared with vacant eyes at the lengthening shadows . . . a bat swooped low above him. The town was a picture of silence and desolation.

Coarse weeds and brush grew in the street, and where the boardwalk had broken through, weeds had filled the spaces. Here and there glass lay upon the walk as it had fallen from a broken window. Several of the windows had been boarded up, and the hitch rail was down, lying in the street. The old signs were weathered and faint.

He walked his horse slowly up the street, staring from sign to sign. Memories flooded back. . . .

Buell's Bank . . . that one would have to come down. *Susan Brown's Hats, Shoes & Notions* . . . *Assay Office* . . . *Yankee Saloon* . . . *Veitch Hotel: Room & Board* . . . *Deming's Emporium* . . . *General Merchandise* . . . *Pearly Gates' Saloon & Dance Hall* . . . *Mom Jelks's Home-Made Pies, Cakes & Bread* . . . *Blacksmith Shop* . . . There were others, some almost illegible.

Riding back down the street, he searched for and found Deming's ladder, which he had once used long ago, and removed the sign from Buell's Bank, carefully breaking it up for kindling.

There was no sign on the long bunkhouse that had offered bunks to those less discriminating than the hotel patrons. Not far from it was the jail, blasted from solid rock, and boasting three iron-barred cells. It was a gloomy place but, so far as he remembered, it had never been used.

He led his horse to the reservoir back of the Yankee Saloon, a tank built of stone some sixteen feet across and, as he recalled, about eight feet deep. A thin trickle of water ran from the tank, and a somewhat larger trickle ran into it.

He led the black to the water and let him drink, then after a few minutes led him back down the street and tied him near the Yankee Saloon. With the butt of his Winchester he smashed the hasp from the saloon door and pushed it open.

It was still light enough for him to see that the mirror behind the bar was intact, and that there were several rows of glasses and empty bottles. In the back a dim stairway led to a balcony, where cavernous doorways opened to several rooms.

Chairs and tables still stood in the room, and poker chips were scattered about, a few playing cards among them. Dust lay thick over everything, and cobwebs hung everywhere. A folded newspaper lay beside a cup and saucer on one of the back tables. In a corner sat a pot-bellied stove. He opened the stove door and could feel no draft down the chimney. No doubt birds had nested there.

When he stepped outside his boots echoed on the boardwalk. The sun was gone now, and gloomy shadows gathered between the buildings and in the lee of the mountain. Those great empty eyes of the windows stared down upon him.

The short boom had brought capital to the town. Several moneyed men, anxious to realize on such a boom as the Comstock, had been among the first to rush in. It was one of these who had built the hotel and the Yankee Saloon.

When the crash came and the people fled, disappointed and angry, they left all behind that they could not easily carry. Dishes, glassware, books, papers, odds and ends of clothing—all were left behind. They had fled as if in a hurry to be free of any evidence of their gullibility.

A vagrant breeze skittered a dry leaf along the walk—the only movement in this silent place.

He was a fool, a fool to attempt what he had in mind, yet what else was there? If those people in the wagons were trapped by circumstances, he was trapped, too.

He had worked at many things. He had been a buffalo hunter, a cowhand, trail driver, miner, stage driver, shotgun guard—none of them for long. Longest of all he had been a gambler.

He glanced at the reflection of himself in a darkening window. His eyes could make out no detail, but he knew what was there. A tall man, lean of body, wide of shoulder; a narrow, triangular face, high cheekbones and a strong jaw. On his jaw a bullet scar gave his face a somewhat piratical cast. A tall man wearing a black, flat-brimmed hat and a black frock coat; but Fallon saw more than that: he saw in that vague reflection a shadow, the shadow of failure.

Back down the line somewhere there had been dreams, ambitions, even certainties. Success had been only just around the corner, tomorrow . . . now where was it? Cynically, and without self-deception, he regarded that shadow in the window. That was Macon Fallon, drifter, gambler, ne'er-do-well, staking his last chance on a town that was as big a fraud as he was himself.

What had Ginia said? That he was a sham. Well, she was right. There was nothing to him beyond that, yet . . . suppose he could get a stake here? He could go to San Francisco, open a small business of his own, find a house somewhere, settle down. He could go to the theater, read books . . . he could be a gentleman.

It all depended on what happened here. He must, from these empty shells, create the image of a living, breathing town. He must make those claims appear worked, and he must play upon the imaginations of his possible customers.

Long after dark he heard the wagon rumble across the bridge and turn into an area just outside of town. There they drew up, and there they unyoked the oxen. Ginia rode up the street to meet him.

"Your town doesn't amount to much," she said.

"What did you expect of a ghost town? Gaslight and red carpets?"

Blane came up to them. "Depressing," he said gloomily. "I don't like it."

"It's all right, Pa. It will look better by daylight. You'll see."

It was evidence of her influence that he accepted her reassurance and walked back to the wagon.

"Pa's down," Ginia said worriedly. "I never saw him like this before."

Macon Fallon removed his hat and let the cool air of evening stir around his temples. "Did you ever put yourself in his place?" he asked. "There's a man with a wife and family. He's brought them two-thirds the way across a continent—to what? Your pa," he added, "is no longer a boy. And he's starting all over, in a new country, with almost nothing. He's scared, Miss Blane, and he has a right to be."

"And you?"

Fallon shrugged. "Believe me, no man knows what it means to be scared until he has to think of others besides himself . . . those he's supposed to care for and protect. A man with a wife and family has, in the words of Francis Bacon, given hostages to fortune."

"And you?" she repeated. "Have you given no hostages to fortune?"

"I'm a man alone," he replied shortly, "a man with nothing to add up but a column of wasted years."

Deliberately, he started his horse toward the others, and she rode beside him.

A campfire had been started, and Blane stood beside it, talking. "I don't like leaving that boy back there alone, but these oxen are too tuckered for that trip tonight."

"I thought young Damon stayed with him?" Fallon said.

Al Damon looked up from where he lounged beside the fire. "He'll do all right by himself. I didn't want to wait back there by that damn' wagon."

Blane started to speak, but young Damon was looking at Fallon belligerently. "What's the matter? Don't you like it?"

Fallon stifled a sudden burst of temper. After all, he needed these people.

"There have been Indians around, and for that matter it is somewhere in this area where the Bellows outfit have been raiding wagon trains. Somebody should certainly be back there with that boy tonight, so when I have watered my horse again, I'll ride back."

"You're tired," Ginia objected, "and your horse is, too. You've come a long way, mister."

Their eyes met across the fire. He was tired, and he was impatient, too. He would have liked to reach down and pick up that Al Damon and slap some sense into him.

"No matter," he said. "I'll go."

He could not resist a parting comment, and when he was in the saddle he turned and glanced at Al. "Have a pleasant evening," he said coolly.

Ginia came after him. "I'm sorry," she said. "Al's not the nicest person in the world, and lately he's been worse. Ever since he started wearing that gun."

"Keep them out of the town tonight," he warned. "The floors are old and there's wreckage lying about. Too many chances of snakes, or a bad fall."

He started to turn his horse, then added, "If young Damon wears that gun out here he'd best grow up to it. When a man packs a gun he's supposed to handle the responsibility that goes with it."

Ginia had started to move away, but she turned back. "I'll keep them in camp." She looked into his eyes. "You do your part, and I'll do mine. You'll see that."

After the black horse had drunk again at the reservoir Fallon started back down the road. The stars were out, the night was velvet soft, and there was a faint breeze off the mountains. Around the town the mountains were as bare as mountains of the moon, but farther back there must be trees, for sometimes he almost believed he could smell the pines. However, there was more tangible evidence, for in the wash that ran past the bench and half around it, there were logs, battered trunks of trees carried down by the flash floods. Someday he would find that forest, if forest there was.

As he rode past the camp he heard Al Damon's voice. "Aw, whatya expect? Why does it need two of us back there? I wanted some coffee, and Jim, he said never mind."

Pausing on the rise from which the town was visible, Fallon looked back. It was swallowed in darkness now, with only the tiny red eye of the campfire winking as people passed between himself and it.

That flat below the town—if that wash could be dammed up to hold what water came in those flash floods, a man might irrigate enough to make a crop on that bench. He chuckled at himself. "Still a farmer at heart, Macon. You'll never outgrow it."

How far back was that farm? Seventeen years? And before that, a hazy recollection of white rail fences and a great white house with columns and a graveled drive. That was the plantation his father had inherited, and on which he was born.

His father had inherited slaves, too, and he did not hold with slavery, so he freed them all. Without slaves the plantation could not be worked, and he soon discovered that in freeing slaves he had not only given up a large part of his wealth but the friendship of his neighbors as well. They were slaveholders, and resented his act. Not one of them would make an offer for his land, and when it was finally sold it brought a tenth of its value.

His father had known a lot about land, but nothing about the management of money, and the small farm in Missouri had scarcely paid for itself.

Macon's brother Patrick had been killed by night riders when Macon was twelve, but Macon put a bullet through the skull of one of them as they rode off. With young Patrick dead, the heart went out of his father. Locusts got the crop one year, frost the next. And then one night Colonel Patrick Fallon heard a man boast that it was he who had killed young Patrick. The Colonel named him for a skulking murderer and a coward, and died with the man's bullet in him.

Three nights later the killer of two Fallons met the third—by that time a gangling boy of fifteen whose hands were born with a deftness beyond that of most men. It showed in his handling of cards, and in his use of guns as well.

On that dark road Macon Fallon gave the killer his chance and left him dead, gun in hand, bullet through his belly. And then young Macon Fallon had ridden on to Independence and joined a wagon train for Santa Fe.

Throughout the years that followed, he never lost his interest in land and crops, for it lay deep within his nature. He was Irish first and a farmer second, and both had a love for the land.

He was thinking over this past of his as he neared the wagon. His horse was walking in sand, and he could hear the voices before he came within sight of the men. He heard more than one rough voice, and then a cry of pain.

He drew rein and listened.

"There's women's fixin's in that wagon, so there's got

to be women about." It was a surly, drunken voice. "And I'll take oath there was another wagon here when I first seen you from the bluff yonder."

Another man spoke up. "You tell us what we want to know an' we'll turn you loose."

Fallon walked his horse a few steps farther, going up slope until his eyes could see over the slight knoll that hid the wagon.

Four men stood around the fire, and young Jim Blane had his hands tied behind him. There was a trickle of blood from his lip.

"I'm alone," Jim insisted. "The women's clothes belong to Ma. We're taking them to her in California. There was another wagon, but it went on. When they get to water they'll be coming back for me."

"Don't lie to me, boy. You speak up, or we'll have your boots off and see how much fire your toes will stand."

Macon Fallon slid the Winchester from its scabbard. These were Bellows's men, he knew, and there was no mercy in them.

"Get his boots off, Deke. He'll talk fast enough."

Macon Fallon lifted the Winchester, and when he cocked it the sound was loud in the night. Where there had been voices and movement, there was a sudden silence where nothing stirred.

"Get on your horses, and ride out of here," he said. His tone was conversational, yet all the more deadly for that.

The man standing beside Jim Blane started to lift his rifle, and Fallon shot him through the knee. The man staggered, grasped at his knee, and fell. As one man the others scrambled for their horses.

"You!" Fallon ordered the wounded man. "Get on your horse and get out!"

"He's badly hurt!" Jim Blane protested. "He's bleeding!"

"Back up over here. I'll free your hands."

The outlaw on the ground was groaning and cursing. He was too concerned with his own wound to notice much, but Fallon had no idea where the others were, and had no intention of appearing in the firelight where he might make a good target.

Jim Blane backed into the darkness and Fallon cut the ropes loose with his bowie knife.

"Now disarm that man and get him out of here."

"The man's hurt!" Jim said again.

"He asked for it. You get him out of here. I'll stay out of the light. They might still be around."

When the outlaw was gone, Jim walked back to the fire, carrying the rifle and gun belt. His face was pale with anger. "That was the most cold-blooded thing I ever saw!" he said. "As far as I'm concerned, I want nothing more to do with you!"

Fallon listened into the night with careful attention.

"Stay out of the light," he said, and then he added, "When I came up they were fixing to burn your feet. You seem to have forgotten that."

From the silence that followed it was obvious that in his anger Jim really had forgotten. "They would never have done it," he said after a while. "They were trying to scare me."

"What do you suppose would happen to your ma and your sister if they got hold of them? That was what they wanted to know, wasn't it?"

Jim Blane did not speak. He was still angry, and he did not believe men would do such things, even though these men had been drinking and talked rough.

Fallon explained about the Bellows outfit. They had been riders with Quantrill and Bloody Bill Anderson, and had come west in a body. Disguised as Indians, they had attacked several wagon trains and a few outlying settlements.

Yet even as he spoke, he knew he probably was wasting his time. To those who have lived a sheltered life, exposed to no danger or brutality, only the actual sight of something of the kind will convince. Each person views the world in the light of his own experience.

"They found an old miner," Fallon went on, "who was supposed to have some hidden gold. They tortured him for hours until he died, and a friend of mine who found the body was sick after seeing it."

"I can't believe that."

"Your choice." Fallon leaned back against a boulder and put his Winchester across his lap. "Blane, I'm going to tell you something once, and never again. This is a different country than you're used to, so I'll let that comment ride, because you're so damned ignorant."

Blane turned sharply, but Fallon continued. "You imply out here that a man is a liar, and you'd better be ready to draw a gun. We don't stand for that kind of loose-mouthed talk."

"I think—"

"I don't give a damn what you think."

Fallon got up and walked to his horse. Stripping off the saddle and bridle, he put on a hackamore and picket-rope, then he rubbed the exhausted animal down with handsful of grass, talking to it meanwhile. The horse was worth a dozen men as a sentinel, for even an exhausted mustang, bred in the wild, would sense anything that came close.

When Fallon walked back to where Jim Blane was, he saw the boy was asleep. He looked down at him thoughtfully. A husky, nice-looking kid, and he would learn. They all had to learn, only some of them didn't last long enough.

Awakening with the first gray light, Fallon went to the wagon and found the coffee. When young Jim opened his eyes the coffee was ready, and so was some bacon.

"Eat up," Fallon advised. "They'll be coming soon."

"Pa won't be here for hours. He won't start until it's light."

"He's on his way now. He should be here in about twenty minutes."

Jim went to the water barrel and splashed water on his face and hair. He combed his hair and came back to the fire.

The sky was cloudless, the dry lake on whose edge the wagon stood was a blank waste of grayish white, touched only here and there along the edges with gray brush, heavily coated with dust. In the morning light the mountains looked dark and somber.

Macon Fallon looked sourly at the hills. His every instinct told him to get away from here, to get away as quickly as possible. Whatever else the Bellows outfit knew, they must not be allowed to know how weak the party was. For Bellows and his men thrived on weakness.

Jim Blane filled his cup and looked a challenge at Fallon, who ignored him.

"I find that idea ridiculous," Jim said, "shooting a man simply because he says he doesn't believe you."

"You'll be surprised how little anybody will care what you think. When you live in a country you conform to the customs of that country or you get out. You will discover that most customs originate in response to a need, and there are good and sufficient reasons for that attitude out here."

As he talked he saddled the black horse, his eyes busy with the trail and the ridges around; he looked at the dim track over which the oxen would be coming. It was light enough to see for some distance, and he had long ago seen the faint plume of dust caused by the moving oxen.

"In this country," he added, "a man cannot exist if he is known to be either a coward or a liar.

"Business is done solely on a man's word. Thousands of head of cattle are paid for simply on the seller's statement that there are that many. No signatures, no legal documents, nothing beyond the word of the seller. But when those cattle are finally counted, the count had better be right.

"If a man's word is no good, nobody will do business with him. If he has the reputation of being unreliable he will be treated with contempt or ignored.

"Moreover, few activities in this country are free of danger, and when a man goes into danger he wants to be sure that those who are with him will stand with him through whatever comes. Therefore no man will have anything to do with a known coward.

"If a man starts to drive cattle a thousand miles, more or less, through Indian country, he can expect shooting trouble. He can expect a dozen other occasions to arise, sometimes so many as that in one day, where nerve is required, and he cannot afford to be teamed with a coward.

"Give a man the name of being either a coward or a liar, and he will be lucky to get a job swamping in a saloon."

Fallon stepped into the saddle. "And that is why either of those words, or any implication of them, is a deadly insult and is treated as such.

"You'll find when trouble comes out here you don't run for the law—you settle it yourself, and you're expected to. As a matter of fact, there's rarely anybody to run to for help.

"I think you're a nice kid, so if I were you I'd keep my mouth shut until you find out how things are done. If you do that, you may live long enough to like the country.

"Now keep your rifle handy. You may think those men won't kill. I know they not only will, but they often have, and we haven't seen the last of them. What you want to keep in mind is that they were looking for women, and women in this case means your mother, your sister, and the Damon women."

He did not wait for a reply, and he wanted none. He had taken more time and said more than he usually did and he couldn't imagine why, except—well, Jim Blane did look like a nice kid . . . unlike that Al Damon.

He had ridden only a few minutes when he came up to the oxen. They were coming along slowly, as was their nature, but Blane and Damon were with them, and they were armed.

Fallon reined in and watched them approach the wagon.

That Bellows man had mentioned watching from a bluff, and undoubtedly somebody watched now. The question was, how long would they wait?

When he put out his sign he would be asking for trouble. And he must face it alone.

CHAPTER 2

MORNING CAME TO Red Horse with lemon light in the eastern sky, throwing into sharp relief the old weather-beaten buildings, aged by wind and sun; the warped doors, the faded and scarcely legible signs that overhung the street.

The town was still, the hollow rooms without sound. Far up the street, beyond where the reservoir lay, a road runner raced into view, teetered briefly on top of a boulder, then vanished from sight.

Macon Fallon sat on his black horse and looked up the street.

Could he do it? Dared he even try? Could he lift this town from the sleep of years and make it suddenly take on a bloom of activity? The first arrival might expose the whole shoddy affair, for any chance comer might be one of those who had known Buell's Bluff in its brief heyday.

What he planned was a swindle, and up to now it had not been in him to swindle anyone. Yet he had to keep in mind that what he needed was a stake, enough money to establish himself somewhere, to locate and stock a ranch, to buy land.

He was tired, suddenly very tired, of playing cards in cheap, dirty saloons and listening to the drunken babble of men who should know better. This town was his chance, his one big chance.

Why worry about what would happen to whoever bought his gold claims? They would be adult, in possession of as many senses as he was. They could look around. They would not be forced to buy.

What difference could it make to the Blanes, the Damons, and their like—the people he would use for window-dressing for his scheme? Had he not stopped them, some of them would have died out there on the Sink where others had died before them. Here at least, they had a chance. Or did they?

He studied the town with care. First, he must give to this shabby, deserted town an appearance of prosperity. He must open the Yankee Saloon for business. He must open Deming's Emporium. Blane, he had learned, had once been a blacksmith, and he might be talked into returning to his former trade.

He would clean the brush out of the street, set up a new hitching rail, clean the stone reservoir, repaint the signs along the street. He could trim up some of the trees, and might even transplant some desert flowers to give the town a more homey touch.

The site was excellent, even picturesque. Nature had artfully arranged the trees, and he knew just what needed to be done to give the town the look he wanted.

The signs were almost erased by wind, rain, and blown sand, but at the edge of the dry lake he had seen some iodine weed growing—it was sometimes called inkweed. From this the Indians made a black dye for decorating pottery and blankets, and he could use it on the signs.

He knew the claims people were likely to buy, those unknown for whom he baited his trap. He knew which claims had the best outward indications, and it was these he would stake for himself. Once staked, he would do a bit of work on each so the dumps would have a fresh look to them; and then, once he had sold those claims, he would be down the trail as fast as his horse could carry him.

Damon had kept store before this, and he had brought with him a small stock of goods: he had a few dozen bolts of cloth, clothing of the rougher sort, tools, nails, scissors, needles, thread, and such odds and ends. No doubt the Blanes could find something they could add to the stock.

The food supplies in the wagons would last a couple of weeks if pieced out with meat; after that they must secure supplies, perhaps by barter, from travelers.

He knew that there used to be deer and Big Horn sheep in the mountains, and with luck he could bring in some game. He wanted to look back up that wash, anyway.

Turning in his saddle, he looked again at the flat below the town. In his mind's eye he saw it waving with corn, with planted crops. There was good grazing there now, of the rougher sort, but with water that flat would be transformed. Tomorrow he would ride down and choose a spot for a dam.

Now he rode up to the Yankee Saloon and dismounted, trailing his bridle reins. He went inside for a quick, daylight survey of the premises. Then he took the black horse around back where the trickle from the reservoir watered a small patch of grass. He picketed the horse there and went back inside.

In the mop closet he found a broom and, opening the two doors and the one window that could be opened, he swept out the place. When he had finished sweeping he built a fire out back and put water on to boil in a big black kettle.

Little but personal possessions had been taken away. It was as if the few inhabitants had not wanted anything to hamper their departure. Travel across the Sink was a trial in any case, and nobody wanted a heavy load. It was simpler to leave everything behind.

Macon Fallon glanced at himself in the mirror with a wry expression. He had always told himself work was for fools, and here he was, taking the biggest job he had ever encountered and, surprisingly enough, he was enjoying it.

"When a man gets to enjoying hard work," he said to himself, "he ought to shoot himself." But he did not feel that way.

The sound of footsteps made him turn his head, and he saw Ginia Blane and Ruth Damon. He straightened up from his work.

"You may tell your father the store is across the street, Miss Damon. Your father can clean it up and open with whatever he has to put on the shelves."

He glanced at Ginia, although he had hoped it would not be necessary. She made him uncomfortable. "If your father wishes to repair that wheel he will find tools in the blacksmith shop. I hope he will see fit to go into business there."

"What are you going to do?" Ginia asked, too politely. "Shoot people?"

"Your brother doesn't approve of me, Miss Blane, and neither do you. How fortunate for me that it does not matter. However," he added, "no matter what your brother believes, had I not come along he would now have two badly burned feet."

Ginia Blane had heard chiefly the remark that it did not matter what she thought, and she had not expected that. Like most very pretty girls, she was accustomed to men making an effort to please her. Most of the boys or men she had known would have been embarrassed by her sarcasm, and even had they been ready with a sharp reply, they would not have made it. To be brushed aside so easily irritated her.

"I'm sure," she said stiffly, "that nothing you do will have the slightest interest for me."

"Good!" he said cheerfully. "Now, unless you want to become dishwasher in a saloon, I suggest you run along and play."

Her mouth opened, but the words would not come; so turning sharply on her heel, she led the way across the street.

She was furious. She told herself that never, never under any circumstances, would she speak to him again.

While the water was heating, Fallon assembled all the glasses and bottles he could find, and cleaned out the sink. Next, he found a barrel, tightened the hoops as best he could and filled the barrel with water. Promptly water ran in streams from all the cracks but, given time, it would swell tight.

Wherever he went he kept his Winchester beside him, taking it from room to room as he worked, or as he studied the work to be done. When he needed that rifle he would need it fast, and he was under no illusions about Blane or Damon. They would not realize the necessity to help him until it was too late. They had lived in a far tamer world than his. But he could not complain about their work. With the exception of Al Damon, they all pitched in and worked hard.

Dividing his time between the saloon and the street, Fallon worked from before daylight until after sundown. Stripped to the waist, his lean, powerful body bronzed by the sun, he removed the brush and weeds from the street, and made a sprinkler out of an old can and tried wetting it down.

Ginia looked at him and sniffed. "You seem to forget," she said primly, "there are ladies present."

"If it offends you to see a man peeled to his belt," he said, "I suggest you get over it while you have the time."

By sundown of the second day he was pruning the trees. He had already knocked together a window box and transplanted some desert flowers in it.

On the third day he rode out to the trail and put up his sign.

RED HORSE
6 MILES

Then he returned to the place where he had first seen the faded Buell's Bluff sign and, after gathering some inkweed from alongside the dry lake, he brought the broken-up sign back to town and burned it.

When he had mixed up his color from the inkweed, he went along the street touching up the signs, not only at Damon's store and the blacksmith shop, but at other places, too.

Al Damon saw him doing this and asked, "What's the idea of that? Ain't nobody to run them places."

"There will be," Fallon replied shortly. Al Damon was the one person in the group he did not like; he had not liked him from the first day when he had shirked his job of staying with Jim Blane at the wagon.

Ginia Blane stopped by again. She had watched him mix up the inkweed, and now she watched him lettering the signs. "Where did you learn something like that?" she asked. "I mean that you could get dye from that plant?"

"An Indian couldn't go to a corner store, so he used what lay about him." He gestured at the hills. "There's food and medicine out there, too, if you know what to look for."

"If somebody doesn't show up soon, you may need to know things like that. Our supplies won't last forever." And she moved away.

He had already staked two claims, both of which had had a good bit of work done on them during the former operation. Now, the signs finished, he went to work with a pick and shovel, throwing more waste out on the dump to give it the fresh look of recent mining.

The ground looked good—no question about that. Yet how many such holes in the ground had he seen? How many samples had he examined, those carefully selected samples every miner shows when talking of his claim? Always the rich samples were chosen, the best instead of the average.

He walked back into the drift, studying the formation. He had worked a little in mines, understood only a little, but this did look good. He tried a few pans, but found no color.

On the third day he had killed a deer and a mess of blue quail . . . on the fifth day, a Big Horn sheep. And he had brought in a mess of squaw cabbage and some wild onions.

"Stake claims," he advised the group, "whether you work them or not. You can always sell them with a nice profit when others begin to come."

"And what if you sell a mining claim where there's no gold?" Ginia asked.

"If I knew there was gold there, I'd keep it myself," he replied bluntly. "There are always some who want to take their chances on a claim."

"And you wouldn't care if they found anything or not?"

"Why should I? Am I my brother's keeper?"

No question about it, Ginia Blane was against him, and the farther he stayed away from her the better. Jim Blane did not even speak to him.

On the seventh day four wagons rolled in. They did some trading with Damon, and Blane repaired a wheel, but they did not stay. They had nothing in their minds but California.

Later that day Fallon killed a deer and was riding back into town when he saw a strange horse tied at the hitching rail in front of Damon's store.

Touching the black with a spur, he drummed across the bridge and up the street. As he reached the store, a man came out.

He was a wiry, slender man with insolent eyes. He stopped on the boardwalk and started to roll a cigarette. He wore a tied-down gun and there was a rifle in the boot on the saddle. There was a canteen, but no blanket roll and no saddlebags.

"Live around here?" Fallon asked.

The taunting eyes surveyed Fallon with care as the man touched his tongue to his cigarette, and then drawing his fingers along it, he said, "Down the road a piece."

"I didn't figure you'd come far," Fallon replied pointedly, his glance shifting to the man's horse.

The man looked around, getting out a match. "Red Horse? Now, that's odd. I don't recall ever hearing of such a town around here."

"You have now."

The man took his time with the match, his eyes noting Fallon's gun. "You'll be this Fallon gent . . . Macon Fallon. The name has a familiar sound."

"So does Bellows."

The man chuckled. "You lay it right on the line, don't you? Well, I'm not Bellows, although he did suggest I drop around and offer our services."

"They aren't needed."

"Bellows will decide that." Coolly, he looked around. "Seems to me there's only four or five of you here. That's not very many, is it?"

Fallon stepped down from his horse. "Do you see that bridge down there, my friend? You tell Bellows that every man he sends to Red Horse—every one who doesn't die with lead in him—will hang from that bridge.

"You can also tell him that if he sends so much as one man down here to make trouble, I'll come after him."

"You're carrying a high hand there, friend. It sounds like you're running a bluff."

Fallon felt anger mounting within him. Also, he knew that at the first sign of weakness the Bellows outfit would come down upon them.

"You're wearing a gun," he said.

The man looked at him thoughtfully, his eyes suddenly wary. "I'd say that sounds like you're pretty sure of yourself." He shook his head. "I'll not call, Mr. Fallon."

Standing on the street, Fallon watched the man ride

slowly out of town, and then he turned on his heel and went into the store.

"Another customer," Damon said cheerfully, "bought tobacco."

Fallon indicated his hip. "Where's your gun?"

"Gun?"

"Look," Fallon said, showing his irritation, "that man you just had in here is a killer. He's one of the Bellows outfit. You put on a gun and wear it, and you be ready to use it."

"Seems like tomfoolery to me," the older man said testily. "I never heard of any Bellows gang."

"Nor I," Jim Blane said. "I think those men out on the road were just passing through."

"If it wasn't for your womenfolks I'd ride out of here and let you take the consequences. You people think of the West as if it was Philadelphia."

He rode away, and Damon shrugged. "What's he so touchy about? That seemed a right nice feller. Pleasant as all get out."

"Mr. Damon," Ginia interposed, "maybe he's right. After all, they did tie Jim up, and they hit him."

"They were drunk!" Jim scoffed. "Just drunken cowhands carrying on. There was no need to shoot that man like he did, no need at all."

Ginia walked up the street. Dislike him as she would, there was no getting around the fact that he had worked harder than any of them, and he had asked for no help in cleaning up the street, painting the signs, or repairing the boardwalk.

Not that she trusted him . . . not one bit. But so far as she could see, he had not lied.

He was polishing glasses when she walked into the saloon. "I don't know why you do that. You've nothing to sell."

He gestured toward the barrel. "You underestimate me. That's full of whiskey. Indian whiskey, I'll admit, but whiskey."

"But where could you get it?"

"It depends on what a man has handy, but the formula was worked out by the Indian traders back along the Missouri. Your mother had two gallons of prune juice that had fermented, and she was going to throw it out. I started with that. Then I shaved up a pound of rank black chewing tobacco and a couple of pounds of red peppers. I boiled them together to get the strength out of the tobacco and the peppers. Mrs. Damon had a bottle of Jamaica ginger, so I added that. I dumped it all into forty gallons of spring water, added two bars of soap to give it a bead, and a gallon of black molasses."

"People will drink *that*?"

"It's the only whiskey in town."

"I just don't understand you, Mr. Fallon. Why, that would kill a man!"

"Not the men out here. I promise you, some of them will like it, others will tolerate it."

She frowned, her eyes searching his face. "Mr. Fallon, just what are you trying to do?"

"It should be obvious. I'm playing midwife to a town. Red Horse never really lived, so I'm giving it a second chance."

"And then what?"

He shrugged. "Who knows? The chances are I'll go on to somewhere else."

———

FALLON NO LONGER ate with the Damons and the Blanes. Young Jim Blane obviously disliked him, and some of this feeling seemed to have rubbed off on the others. When he killed meat he shared it with them, then went on about his business.

He had scouted the flat below the town. There was just enough grade to permit an easy flow of water if he could get water on the upper part of the flat. The bed of the wash offered at least one very good site for a dam . . . a narrow place where the walls and bottom were rock for a short distance.

He had rolled a few stones into position across the wash, then with his rope he had snaked a couple of logs down.

Each time he rode out from town he scouted for tracks, but found none. The stock was grazing in a small herd on the lower part of the flat, with Al Damon herding.

Restlessly, Fallon watched the trail each day, but he saw no wagons, no movement at all, and time was running out. Their slim food supply was steadily growing less, and this in spite of his contributions of meat. He himself was living on meat, squaw cabbage, wild onions, and whatever else he could glean from the desert around.

The canyon itself, the dark maw opening into the mountains beyond and behind the town, intrigued him. The walls reared up suddenly just a few hundred yards beyond the last building, but you could not see more than fifty feet into the canyon from the best vantage point the town had to offer.

If a man was caught in that canyon by a flash flood he would simply have no chance at all.

On the eleventh day a wagon showed up, rumbling

over the bridge and into the town. Fallon rode out to meet it.

The driver of the wagon was a lean, hard-faced man who wore a belt gun and had a rifle beside him, leaning against the seat. The woman beside him was motherly-looking, and her face showed strength.

Joshua Teel was from Missouri, a harness-maker by trade, and Fallon took an instant liking to him.

"If you're interested in mining," Fallon said to him, "there are claims to be had; but if you're a harness-maker, why not work at your trade and prospect in your spare time?"

"Injuns about?"

"Used to be, but not since we've been around. Not even any sign." At the risk of losing a prospective citizen, he added, "Frankly, you look like a man I'd like to have on my side. The Bellows outfit is around, and they're as bad as any Indians."

"Heard of them."

Teel cast a glance at the town, letting his eyes sweep slowly around. "Woman's tired of movin', young uns're sickly. Figured to stop for a mite."

"Ever farm any?"

Teel's eyes showed a mild interest. "Raised to it. Taken my first steps behind a plow."

Macon Fallon explained about the flat, and the dam he had begun. The Missourian listened, his eyes straying from the flat to Fallon's face from time to time.

"You shape like a gamblin' man," he said at last, "but you talk like a man who'd made hay. I'll look at it."

The following day, Fallon went to the wash and worked the entire day, sunrise to sunset, on his dam. At the beginning, one would hardly have recognized it as a dam, for what he was doing was building a barrier that would catch other debris and pile it up. Nobody from the town came to see what he was doing, and none offered to help.

On the day that marked the end of the second week, four wagons stopped and business was brisk. One of the wagons pulled up at the Yankee Saloon. It was followed by another wagon driven by a burly Negro.

The driver of the first wagon came into the saloon, a stocky man with a shock of prematurely gray hair and the beginnings of a paunch. He had a smooth, rosy-cheeked face and keen blue eyes.

"Brennan's the name," he announced. "I'll have a whiskey."

As Fallon poured the glass, Brennan added, "I'm a saloon man myself. Maybe I could offer some suggestions."

"I'm sure you could," Fallon replied dryly, "so let me offer one. Don't drink the whiskey."

Brennan glanced at him, then tasted the drink. Carefully, as if fearful it might explode, he replaced the glass on the bar. "Unusual flavor," he said politely. "I don't believe I recognize the brand."

"Indian whiskey. My own version."

"If you don't mind, I'll have a glass of water."

He tasted the water, then put the glass down, smiling. "Limestone water, the purest there is . . . just like from the hills of Bourbon County, Kentucky. My friend"—he gestured toward the water—"if you really want to make good whiskey, there's the first essential . . . good water."

Fallon walked around the bar. "Mr. Brennan, I don't want to make whiskey. I don't want to operate a saloon. I'll supply the water and whatever equipment you need, and I'll handle the gambling, if there is any. You operate the saloon and we split fifty-fifty . . . how's that?"

Brennan tasted the water again. "Sixty-forty," he said. "I have operated saloons in New York, Richmond, Louisville, Abilene, Leadville, Corinne, and Silver Reef. I know my business."

Fallon looked at him, then out across the flat. Brennan was perhaps thirty-five, and a man who appreciated the good things of life, if Fallon was any judge. Yet here he was, though the towns showed a steady progression westward . . . why?

"You've made a deal. Take over as of now. Tomorrow we'll scout the location for a still."

"You aren't going to ask any questions?"

"If you're the man who can handle the job, I want you. If you are not, out you go."

"I killed a man," Brennan said.

"If the Bellows outfit decide to raid us," Fallon said bluntly, "you may have to kill several."

"This is my town," Brennan said quietly, "and I'm glad to be home."

Brennan, among other things, had three barrels of whiskey in his second wagon. He also had a case of claret and approximately a hundred empty beer bottles. What else he carried was not immediately obvious. They divided the upstairs into two apartments and Brennan moved into one of them.

Slowly, business picked up. Several wagons came by, and once a whole wagon train drove in and camped the night on the upper flat. Fallon was always around, but each day he worked some upon the dam. Twice, Joshua Teel joined him, bringing his mules to help, and slowly the dam grew.

IT WAS MIDAFTERNOON, and Fallon was sitting at a table in the saloon drinking coffee when Al Damon came in. He walked to the bar and lifted a boot to the brass rail. He wore a pair of new Spanish-style boots with high heels and Mexican spurs. His gun, which he had taken to wearing when he began herding cattle, was tied down.

"Gimme a whiskey." His tone indicated that he half expected to be refused the drink and was prepared to make an issue of it.

"Two bits a shot," Brennan said. "Most places it's less, but whiskey is hard to come by out here."

Al Damon slapped a silver dollar on the bar. "You think I ain't got it?" he demanded. "Now give me that drink."

Brennan served him without comment and held the whiskey up to see the light through the amber liquid.

"Are you still herding the stock?" Fallon asked mildly.

"Sure. What of it?"

"Who's with them now?"

"Aw, they're all right. What's to bother them?"

"The Bellows crowd might run them off."

Al Damon turned his back to the bar and rested his elbows on it; a heel hung over the brass rail. "You're makin' a big thing out of them," he said sarcastically. "What would a high-powered outfit like that want with a bunch of old work oxen?"

"High-powered?" Fallon repeated. "That outfit? There isn't guts enough in the crowd to tackle a bunch of grown men. Not unless they outnumber them five to one."

Al put his glass down so hard he spilled whiskey. "A lot you know! That's a tough outfit!"

Fallon ignored the comment and glanced out the door, a frown gathering over his eyes. He started to ask a question, then thought better of it.

At the bar Al was saying to Brennan, "Pa says you tended bar in Abilene. Was Hickok there when you were?"

"Yes."

"I hear tell he was slick with a gun. Why, they do say he was the fastest of all them outlaws!"

"He wasn't an outlaw. He was the town marshal."

"*Wild Bill* Hickok? I figured him for an outlaw for sure."

"Very few outlaws are gunfighters," Brennan said. "As for Hickok, those of us who knew him liked him for other reasons than his skill with weapons."

"What about that there Clay Allison? Wasn't he an outlaw?"

"He ranches down around Cimarron. He's no outlaw."

Fallon finished his coffee and refilled his cup. "One thing it takes to make a gunfighter," he commented, "that no amount of practice will give you."

Al Damon turned belligerently. "What's that?" It was quite obvious that he had no liking for Fallon.

"Guts enough to look at a man who is shooting at *you,* and shoot back. I've seen many a would-be gunfighter act big and brave until suddenly he actually gets into a gun battle with a grown man who's cold sober. Then they turn yellow as saffron."

Al Damon, at nineteen, had fallen into a familiar pattern. He had decided that he was unique, something very special. Without having tested it, he decided he was the material of which gunfighters are made. He had tied down his gun, had taken to swaggering and talking tough. The one fact that so far had not impressed itself on his consciousness was that when a man wears a gun he is no longer playing games. A gun implies that, if need be, he will shoot. It also implies that if circumstances so develop, he may be shot at.

Macon Fallon was deeply disturbed, but he did not wish it to show. Nobody had a corner on being foolish, and he had himself had his foolish moments—but not with a gun.

Gunfighters were created by circumstances, not by deliberate choice. Once they had the reputation, they often worked hard to become better at it, but that was simply self-preservation. Nobody in his right mind wanted the name of gunman.

In a country where all men wore guns and where it was the accepted manner of settling disputes, a few were sure to be gifted with a little more skill, a little more nerve; and surviving, they became known as gunfighters.

Most of the gun battles he knew of had been over nothing important. Like that one at Seven Pines.

With a shock, Macon Fallon realized he had been so busy repairing and touching up the town that he had completely forgotten Seven Pines. By now the posse, sobered up, might have thought better of lynching. On the other hand, they might have convinced themselves they were right, and might continue to look for him, or to make inquiries.

With all the rest of his troubles, why did Al Damon have to take the notion that he was a gunfighter? Fallon knew what would happen next. Damon would swagger around a bit, but in the back of his mind would be the notion that he had never shot anybody, and that he would not be a real gunfighter until he had.

Fallon finished his coffee and went outside. He could not forget that silver dollar on the bar, or Al's sudden defense of the Bellows outfit. Where had Al picked up that money? He might have brought it west with him . . . but had he?

Inside the saloon, Brennan gestured after Fallon. "There goes a man. A dangerous man."

"*Him?*"

Al's voice was filled with incredulous contempt. "I wouldn't be afraid to take him on myself. He doesn't look so tough to me."

"I've helped bury men who used those same words." Brennan leaned his hands on the bar. "Kid, you've tied on a gun, but did you ever see a man gut-shot? Bleeding to death with his innards in the dust? It doesn't have to be the other man—it can be you. Keep that in mind."

Al gulped whiskey and wiped his mouth with the back of his hand. "What of it?" he said boldly. "I'll likely look on it my ownself."

"And probably they will be your own. I've seen them come and go, kid, and let me tell you something. You aren't one of them. You aren't even the beginning of a gunfighter."

After Al Damon had gone, Brennan cursed himself for a fool. Nothing he could have said would make Al Damon more anxious to prove him wrong. Only, after a time a man became impatient. Each one of these youngsters thought he had discovered something new, and each one was following a trail that had been worn down by those who had gone before, making the same mistakes. What they were seeking was empty and flat, and what they stood to lose was all the warmth and beauty of life, the things worth having that they might never realize; but the things they valued—the food, the drink, the girls, and the reputation—all would be gone like a wisp of smoke . . . and for what?

Brennan went to the street end of the bar, where there was a window that permitted him to see some distance down the street. He had said this was his town, and so he wished it to be. He was tired of moving. He wanted to dig in somewhere and stay there.

Already he had begun to create the world he wanted to keep, and part of it he had brought with him. He liked operating a saloon. He enjoyed selling good whiskey. A quiet man, not talkative himself, he liked conviviality around him, liked the easy talk, the friendliness of men. Drunks he did not like, but he had learned to cope with them.

Brennan had really built for himself two worlds: the world of the saloon, where he worked and earned his keep; and the world of his own rooms when he went upstairs and closed the door behind him. He would not, he told himself, mix with the townspeople . . . that way lay trouble. Like Macon Fallon, he would keep to himself.

He and Fallon rarely talked together; when they did it was usually over coffee in the morning. Brennan had never been inside Fallon's quarters, nor Fallon inside his.

Brennan and his Negro handyman had carried his things upstairs after dark, and arranged them in his rooms. He had a few paintings, and they were good ones, an upright piano, and about fifty books. A customer had given him a copy of Montaigne, and that had started him reading. Twenty years had passed since then...he still had that copy of Montaigne. In one room a Turkish rug was on the floor, and a fine four-poster bed stood against the wall.

Habitually, Brennan kept a Winchester rifle near the window and a shotgun under the bar in the saloon, and he always carried one of his derringers on his person. Other weapons he had cached in likely places.

He had rolled into Red Horse with two wagons containing most of what he had been able to accumulate in all his years up to now, and it was not much. In another sense, he came to Red Horse with a great deal, for most of what John Brennan had gathered was in his own mind.

He was a man who loved the flavor of things—to live life slowly, to enjoy his books, music, paintings, people, and the life around him. He had come to the frontier almost of necessity, but he had remained because he loved it.

John Brennan welcomed all men, was friend to few. He had not formed a definite opinion about Macon Fallon as yet, but he liked him anyway. There was strength in the man, and background, too. It showed in so many little things. It showed in his way of speaking of woman, always with courtesy, never indicating familiarity, always with respect. It showed in the way he ate, the way he drank, the manner in which he carried himself. Brennan was not of the gentry, but he knew gentry when he saw them.

There was one thing in particular about Fallon that Brennan wondered about. Macon Fallon was seeking residents for his town; he made overtures to those with trades—except for miners. In a town whose wealth was supposed to be founded on mining, there were no miners. This was curious, and John Brennan wanted to know why.

Twenty-nine families now lived in Red Horse. The hotel had been opened, a doctor had hung out his shingle, Damon had taken in a partner named Crest, with additional stock. A bakery had opened.

———

BRENNAN WAS AT the bar early in the day that marked the beginning of the town's fourth week. The door opened and Joshua Teel entered.

"Where's the meetin'?" he asked.

"Meeting?"

"Macon Fallon said to meet him here. Said there'd be others."

Brennan jerked his head toward the back room. "Fallon's back there. There's others with him."

He watched the Missourian go into the back room and close the door after him. Odd, that Fallon had said nothing to him. He took out a cigar and clipped the end, staring down the street at nothing at all.

Teel, Riordan, and Shelley . . . all fighting men . . . The door opened, and Devol came in with Zeno Yearly. Brennan again jerked his head to indicate the rear room. He struck a match. He lifted it to light his cigar.

Teel was a veteran of Indian and border fighting, Riordan and Shelley had both been with the Fifth Cavalry. He was not sure about Devol, but Yearly was a trail driver and a Texan.

After the men had gone, Fallon came into the room

and ordered coffee, which Brennan kept ready. "Felt no need to talk to you," Fallon said suddenly. "You told me this was your town, and you stood ready to fight if need be."

"You are expecting trouble soon?"

"Any day." He tasted his coffee and put the cup down. "Blane, Damon, Crest, and some of that lot, they'd talk too much trying to make up their minds, and by that time the town would be burning over their heads, and their women raped or murdered. I want a few men I can count on. I want to know where they are, and how ready they are."

He sipped the coffee again, and then went on. "I think I can handle whatever comes, and they will start with me. What I want is half a dozen men at least who won't get so interested in what I'm doing that they forget to keep watch."

"What about me?" Brennan demanded. "You leaving me out?"

"You stay right where you are. You'll know what to do without me telling you. It seems likely some of them will come in here, and if they do, I'd like them out of action."

Brennan put his cigar on the edge of the bar, carefully, so as not to disturb the ash. "I should like to open a bottle of wine," he said.

" 'Of the first grape only,' " Fallon quoted.

Brennan glanced up from the bottle he had taken from under the bar. " 'A vine bears three grapes,' " he said, " 'the first of pleasure, the second of drunkenness, and the third of repentance.' " He filled two glasses two-thirds full. "I believe it was Anacharsis who said that."

He pushed one glass across the bar to Fallon, then lifted his own. "To Red Horse!" he said.

"Ah? . . . yes . . . yes, of course. To Red Horse!"

But he had hesitated. Brennan, lying that night between white sheets, considered that.

He had hesitated . . . why?

CHAPTER 3

FOUR MEN WERE seated about the fire when Al Damon rode up. The place was a hollow among the rocks and brush not over half a mile from the lower end of the flat. The trail young Damon had followed from the flat to the hollow was invisible from the town itself, and the town was invisible from the hollow. Bellows was there, as they had said he would be, and Tandy Herren.

"Got any news for us, kid?"

Al swung down from the saddle and sauntered up to the fire, supremely conscious of the heavy pistol on his leg. He squatted on his heels and started to roll a cigarette.

"Nobody expects any trouble, if that's what you mean."

"And there won't be any trouble." Bellows winked at the men across the fire. "We just want to have a talk with that man Fallon. The one who runs everything down there."

Al spat. "He doesn't run me. And he ain't about to!"

Luther Semple, who sat beside Bellows, had been a sidehill farmer in the Ozarks when the War between the States broke out. He had no particular interest in the war, but the prospect of loot interested him very much indeed. He joined Quantrill first, then Bloody Bill Anderson, and finally Bellows. He was a lean, sour-faced man who had moved west with Bellows, raiding lonely buffalo hunters' camps or murdering travelers.

"Whyn't you take him on, Al?" Lute said. "Be a feather in your bonnet to kill him."

"He leaves me alone."

"Scairt, that's what he is, he's scairt of you."

Al Damon did not quite believe that, but it sounded good and he wanted them to believe it. "He leaves me alone," he repeated.

"He had no business shootin' up my man like he done," Bellows said. "That man's still laid up."

Tandy Herren said nothing. Al stole a quick glance at him through the smoke of his cigarette. Herren was a lean, wolfish young man only two or three years older than Al himself. He wore two pearl-handled pistols.

Al felt a thrill of excitement go through him as he looked at those guns. Lute had told him Tandy had killed sixteen men.

"Seems to be a lot of comin' and goin' down there," Bellows commented. "Your pa must be doin' a nice business."

"It's that Brennan up at the saloon . . . he rakes it in with both hands."

"Whyn't you promote a dance down there? All those pretty women. You had you a dance, we'd all come a-callin'. Only trouble with outlawin', womenfolks are scarce. Different when you go to town, for they sure fling themselves at you. Fair sets a woman a-sweatin' to get nigh a real honest-to-Charley outlaw."

Tandy Herren glanced at Lute skeptically. "You tell

me. When was the last time you had a woman worked up over you—outlaw or no?"

"It's a fact!" Lute insisted. "An outlaw's reckless an' darin' . . . womenfolks set up an' look at men like that."

Al Damon was uncomfortable. The talk always got around to women, and all he wanted to do was hold up a stage or run off some cows.

"That there Blane filly. Vince, when he was down there to town, he seen her. Said she was really somethin'."

"She's pretty," Al admitted, "but uppity."

He took up the pot and added coffee to his cup. He ought to be getting back. Pa had come down on the flat the other day when he was not there and had raised pure-dee hell about it.

"Here"—Bellows took up a canteen—"try some of this in your coffee. Put hair on your chest."

Bellows dumped a slug of whiskey in Al's cup, and Al choked off his protest. To tell the truth, he didn't really care for whiskey. He drank it because it seemed the thing to do.

"Who's the law down there? Have they got themselves a marshal yet? Or is it vigilantes?"

"Aw!" Al scoffed. "They're a bunch of farmers. Ain't nerve enough for vigilantes. More'n likely Fallon considers himself the law, but he doesn't wear a badge."

Bellows dumped a liberal dose of whiskey into his own coffee. "Seems to me," he said shrewdly, "what you need is an election. You could call yourselves an election and vote Fallon right out. Then you folks could run the town as you please."

Al gulped his coffee and whiskey and felt it burn all the way down. "I dunno. Fallon owns the town. I can't see how we could run him out."

"Who says he owns the town? You ever hear of a man who *owned a town?*"

Al took another swallow of coffee and tried to recall, but failed to recollect anything of the kind. Not that he knew much about towns or their governments. His dislike of Fallon was now given a sense of grievance. After all, why should Pa and the rest of them give him all that money? All he had done was know the town was there and take them to it.

Just wait until he saw Pa! And they all thought they knew so all-fired much! And old man Blane . . . But he would talk to Jim first. Jim Blane did not like Fallon the least bit, nor did Ginia.

If he could throw Fallon out of town, Al was thinking, that would make him a big man.

"If you could get rid of Fallon," Bellows suggested, "you might take over your ownself. You could run the town."

He had not considered that . . . yet, why not? Then his sudden elation vanished. They knew him too well. Blane would laugh at him, and so would Pa. "They seen me grow up," he told himself; "they'd never believe I could do it."

Still, if he got rid of Fallon by himself . . . ?

Bellows seemed to divine what he was thinking. "What if you shot Fallon right out of his job? They wouldn't give you any argument then. Why, you'd be *chief!* You'd be top man!"

There was a distant rumble of thunder, but Al did not notice it. And he had forgotten the cattle.

Bellows got to his feet and kicked dirt on the fire. "Here"—he handed the half-empty bottle to Al—"you finish this. See you next week. One of the boys will drop by and tell you where."

Bellows mounted and then glanced sharply at Al. "Fallon shot one of my men. There'd be a place in my outfit for the man who put a bullet into him." And he added, "I don't care if he's killed or not—I just want him out of action."

They rode away, and Al had another drink and watched them go. He still had not been taken to the hideout, which meant they did not trust him. Well . . . he'd show them!

The sun was still high and hot. He took another drink, and pocketed the bottle. Then he swung into the saddle and started for the flat.

He was not used to whiskey and he had taken on quite a lot, but he was not thinking of that. He was thinking of Fallon. If he could kill Fallon, he could be the boss . . . the marshal, maybe. He would stand on the corner in a black coat, and he would get a pair of pearl-handled pistols like those Tandy Herren wore.

And he'd show that uppity snip of a Ginia Blane!

Suddenly, he came upon a vague sort of trail. It was narrow, no more than six to eight inches wide and very old. Made by Indians, no doubt, or by mountain sheep. He stared at it, let his eyes follow it. Some fifty yards farther along and out in the open on a barren shoulder, it simply vanished, erased by time. But still farther on, away up the slope, it seemed to appear again.

Drunkenly, he stared at the almost invisible trail. Why, this must be the trail he'd heard Fallon wondering about. Fallon had said there were no sheep tracks up the canyon, so they must have another way over the mountains. This could be it.

Turning his mount, he followed the trail for half a mile, picking out bits of it here and there. It was only occasionally visible, and when he finally gave up he had passed the flat, and no thought of cattle was in his mind. Vaguely, he heard a rumble back in the mountains . . . sounded like thunder.

He was very drunk and very sleepy. He drank the last of the whiskey and turned his horse toward town. The sun had disappeared, but he gave it no thought. He dropped the empty bottle beside the ancient trail.

It was not easy to find a way down off the mountain, and it was the horse that found it, and not Al Damon.

That night it rained in the mountains.

Macon Fallon was tired and had gone to bed early. He awoke to the flash of lightning and the sound of thunder. There was a patter of rain on the roof.

Then he sat up abruptly. It was going to rain . . . it was sprinkling even now. The brief patter stilled, and Fallon sat up in bed staring at the window and trying to figure out why he had awakened so suddenly.

The dam!

He tried to think of something that remained undone; but if the water came, he was as ready as he would ever be.

He swung his feet to the floor and went to the window. He looked toward the mountains and could make out the great thunderheads that loomed above them. Lightning lit up a cloud like a huge incandescent globe. As he watched, speculating on what the rain would mean to the town and the crops that had been planted, he saw a rider coming up the street. From the way the man sat his saddle, he was either drunk or hurt.

Sure that the man was injured, Fallon started to turn from the window when lightning flashed again.

It was Al Damon.

"Al Damon?" he said aloud, unbelievingly.

He glanced at his watch. It was past one in the morning and Al should have been in bed hours ago, and the stock in the corrals. Turning swiftly, he went to the back window, which looked toward the corrals. At the flash of lightning he strained his eyes toward them. The corrals were empty!

If the stock was not in its corrals, then the herd must have taken shelter from the approaching storm in its usual place, the undercut bank above the dam. But it was one of the duties of the herdsman to keep the stock from returning to that shelter.

For a quarter of a mile above the dam there was no way of escape from the wash by anything larger than a man on foot or a mountain lion. A flash flood in the mountains, which would surely follow any heavy rainfall there, would drown every head of stock at Red Horse, except for the riding horses kept in the town itself.

Those cattle and horses represented every chance of escape these people had if anything went wrong at Red Horse. To some of them, their stock represented their very existence here, and without it they could not survive.

There was no hesitation in Macon Fallon. He glimpsed the empty corral and, turning swiftly, he grabbed his pants off the chair and stepped into them. In a sudden panic, he stamped into his boots and caught up his gun belt. As he strapped it on, he caught up his hat and slicker and ran for the door.

Brennan, sitting up in bed and reading from Montaigne by a coal-oil lamp, heard the door close, heard the rush of Fallon's feet on the steps. He got out of bed and went to the window. The street below was empty.

He stood there for a minute or two, worrying about what was happening, but reflecting that had Fallon needed him he would have rapped on his door.

Fallon threw the saddle on the black and led him to the door of the stable. Thunder rumbled in the mountains as he stepped into the stirrup. He had always told himself he was a selfish man, and he believed it. So far he had not paused to consider what he was about to do in reference to that belief.

The black was an excellent stock horse, and automatically Fallon felt for the rope at the pommel as he turned the horse into the street.

A dark figure moved in front of the harness shop, working with a shovel. Somebody was ditching in expectation of rain.

"Teel?"

"Is that you, Fallon?"

"Going to check the stock. I could use a hand."

"Got to get my slicker."

Teel wasted no time. Fallon could see him saddling up by the light of a lantern. There was a smell of fresh hay and manure, and Teel moving swiftly in the vague light seemed like a figure in some witchery.

Rain was pouring down upon the mountains when they reached the flat. The Missourian knew as well as Fallon where the cattle sheltered. The town's oxen, some of its horses, and all of the mules and cows were there.

At the cut in the bank Fallon caught Teel's arm. "You stay here to guide them. I'll go down and start them back."

"Two can do it better," Teel said, and started his horse down the cut.

"When the water comes," Fallon shouted above the thunder, "she'll come a-rolling with logs, boulders—everything! You leave it to me!"

Teel ignored him, and went down the bank, with Fallon following. On the bottom they spurred their horses, charging at a dead run along the floor of the wash toward the cattle. At any moment Fallon expected to hear the roar of the flood rushing down from behind them. The hair prickled along the back of his neck.

Several of the oxen and mules were already on their feet, looking nervously toward the mountains. Teel rode into them, slapping with his coiled rope. "*Hi*-yuh! *Hi*-yuh! Git with it now! *Git!*"

Sluggishly, the rest got to their feet. Desperately, yelling and slapping with their ropes, the men got them started. Fallon slid his .44 into his hand and put a bullet into the air. The cattle started to move, but the leaders held back.

"Hike 'em!" Fallon shouted. "The leaders can smell it! Once they hear that water comin', nothing will make them go toward it!"

Firing their guns, yelling, and whipping with their ropes, they started the reluctant herd up the wash. Fallon felt a coolness on his face, and terror swept through him. He knew that feeling . . . he had felt it before. A wall of water was pushing the air before it.

They fired again and again, and the black, stock horse that he was, nipped at the nearest hindquarters. They were moving now, really moving. Lightning flashed and the leaders stopped and started to mill. Fallon drove at them, lashing them into a run.

Rain began to fall. A few scattered drops, large drops hard driven by the wind, and then a roaring rush of rain . . . a regular cloudburst. Lightning struck somewhere ahead, and again the leaders stopped and started to turn. Fallon, leaving the drag to Teel, drove through the herd, whipping the leaders on.

Suddenly, above the crash of thunder and the rushing roar of the rain, they heard another sound. The herd was running good now and Fallon fell back.

"Drive 'em!" he yelled. "It's in the *canyon!"*

With rope and pistol they harried the cattle up the canyon before them, their horses racing back and forth, nipping with their teeth at the frightened creatures. Suddenly Fallon saw, looming ahead, the boulder that marked the cut up which they must drive the cattle.

At the same instant they rounded into a straight stretch of wash that was all of a quarter of a mile long, and even as they turned into the stretch, with the boulder only a few yards ahead, a lightning flash revealed the rolling wall of water.

Twelve feet high, tossing logs on its crest, it came rushing toward them at the speed of an express train. For an instant, Fallon was appalled.

They couldn't make it. There simply wasn't time. This time he'd bought it, and for Josh Teel, too. Then urgency broke through his fear and he screamed.

"Teel!" He tried to make his voice heard above the roar of the storm. "Let's *go-o-o!"*

Teel caught the wave of his arm in the almost continually flashing lightning, and together they broke for the gap. Almost at the same moment, a lead steer saw the gap, too, and recognized the way home. Bawling frightfully, the huge ox started for the gap, and in an instant, all were following. Caught up in the rush, Fallon was swept along, and suddenly, through the bawling of cattle and the roar of the rushing water, he heard a lost, despairing cry.

Even as he was swept upward to safety, he glanced back and saw that Josh Teel was down, his leg pinned under his fallen horse.

He did not think, he did not pause to estimate the risks involved. He might kill the horse, he might hit Teel, but there was only one chance for them. The horse was lying still. He wanted to burn the animal with a bullet, to make it get up or give Teel a chance to free his leg.

Fallon drew his pistol and chopped down, firing as the gun came level. The horse screamed and lunged and, scrambling to its feet, it went for the gap, and made it.

The roaring of the water drowned all other sound, but Teel, free of the horse, threw his body around and grabbed for the rocky wall of the wash. And then the flood rushed upon him and he was submerged, vanishing under the dark, glistening water.

Dropping from his horse, Fallon took the rope from the pommel and rushed to the bank. As he ran, he shook out a loop. Never better than a fair roper, and long out of practice, he knew it was Teel's one wild chance now . . . if the Missourian was not already dead, already swept away.

The wash was filled with the racing water, running ten feet deep, tossing logs and debris. How long would it last? An hour? Two hours? Three? Teel's body would be carried far in that time, carried down the canyon and out upon the desert.

Fallon worked his way toward the edge, watching out for cracks that might tumble him into the wash. Even as he neared the edge, a huge chunk, a dozen feet long and half as wide, was torn from the opposite bank and fell into the stream.

He drew closer to the spot where Teel had vanished. Here, clinging to his loop—the other end was tied fast to the pommel of the saddle—he lay down in the mud and peered over the edge.

Below him was a ghostly white hand, slipping on the wet rock. And below that was Teel's face, barely out of the water; his other hand clinging to the rock with a precarious grip.

All that saved him from the violent current was a shoulder of rock that, projecting scarcely a foot into the stream, broke the current just enough so he had not been torn free. Yet even as Fallon saw him, Teel's fingers began to slip.

Reaching over, Fallon dug his knees into the damp earth to give him purchase, and grasped Teel's wrist.

Slippery . . . too slippery.

With his free hand, depending on the slight grip with his knees to keep him from falling over into the water, Fallon shook out a loop and dropped it. The loop missed, but Teel was no fool. He was a tough man who had fought for life before, and he did not weaken now. Deliberately, he bobbed his head into the noose, then with a quick, desperate look at Fallon, he let go with his other hand and thrust it through the loop.

Instantly his whole weight was on Fallon's slippery wrist-grip, and the movement jerked Fallon's knees loose. His knees skidded in the mud, and with a gasp of panic, Fallon felt himself going over.

Wildly, he grabbed out and caught the rope. It tore through his hand, but his grip held. Then his body struck

Teel's with a thud, and the two men clung together. Fighting for his life against the tug of the current, Fallon got his arm through the same loop with Teel.

Rain beat at their faces with angry fingers, and the rushing water tore at their bodies. Once a heavy chunk of wood struck Fallon in the side and he cried out in pain, but the rope remained taut.

Carefully, Fallon began to feel against the bank for a foothold. If he could just get a little slack in the rope . . .

Teel, who knew as much about roping a horse as Fallon, caught on at once, and dug for a toehold. If they could just get some slack.

They got it, and the black instantly backed up to keep the rope taut, and they had gained a few inches. Again they tried, and Teel got a foothold, although Fallon could get none, but Teel got an arm under Fallon's shoulders and heaved him up enough to get the slack they needed. Promptly the black horse backed up, tightening the rope again.

But that was the end of it.

Only inches above them was the edge, and water swirled about their hips. They could find no foothold. The only consolation was that Fallon knew the black would hold. He would keep that rope tight until he fell from exhaustion.

That black horse had roped too many bad steers, mean longhorns, and bulls that were fighters. It was his job to keep that rope tight, and it was thus he had been trained. He would keep the rope tight until doomsday, and after.

Sagging in the loop, which cut into their bodies, they waited. Fallon's arms ached. His hand, burned on the rope, was raw and bloody, and the pain was frightful.

The great roaring of the water had ceased, but it still rushed around them, still tugged at their bodies; but the awful, tearing violence of it was gone. It was still dangerous, but the black horse was holding them.

"She's fallin'!" Teel shouted in Fallon's ear. "Below my hip pockets now!"

After a few more minutes the fall was obvious. And now, on his right, Fallon saw an outthrust of rock.

Reaching out, he got a foot on it and pushed up; the black horse instantly took up the slack. Fallon swung a hand up and got hold of the edge. Teel's boots fought for a toehold and dug in, and suddenly they both had arms over the edge and the black took up the slack so suddenly that they found themselves over the edge and sprawled in a muddy tangle.

Teel struggled to his feet and stood swaying. "You surely picked a lousy night for a ride!" he said wryly.

Fallon got up and spoke to the black horse, which walked toward them. "I could do with some coffee," he said.

"Hell!" Teel said. "I could do with a drink, although I've sworn off the stuff."

Riding double, they rode back into town.

It was breaking day when they came into the street, covered with mud, and exhausted but hilarious. Damon was out, sweeping off his walk, and he looked at them in astonishment.

"What happened to you two?" he asked.

Teel was not a man given to saving face or mincing words. Briefly, he told what had happened. "We could have lost the herd," he said at the end, "and you've eight or nine head there yourself."

"I can't understand it," Damon said. "Al wouldn't—"

"He was drunk," Pete Shoyer interrupted. Shoyer was a late-comer and owed no loyalty to Damon. "I got up to close a window and saw him ridin' up the street. Chances are he's back there in the stable, sleepin' it off."

———

AL DAMON AWAKENED slowly. The first thing he smelled was the fresh hay beneath him; and opening his eyes, he found himself staring up at the low rafters in the shed behind the store, which served them as a stable.

He rolled over and pushed himself up, sitting back and looking around. His head throbbed heavily and his mouth tasted awful. His pistol had fallen from its holster, and he picked it up and slipped it back in place.

The sun was high in the sky. The morning noises were around him, but they were late noises. No roosters were crowing, but a hen that had laid an egg was cackling.

He got up, then staggered against a doorpost, holding his head.

His horse was gone . . . the saddle was gone. He looked outside and cringed as the sunlight struck his eyes. He'd better find that horse and get the stock out on the grass. Pa would—

The horse was nowhere in the stable, nor was it outside, as he half expected it to be. Hitching up his belt, he put on his hat and went striding angrily into the store.

"Where's my horse?" he demanded. "Somebody rode off on my horse."

His father looked up. "The horse you call yours," he said coldly, "belongs to Blane, and Jim Blane is riding it now. He also has your job of riding herd on the stock."

Al Damon was feeling mad, but his father intervened before his son could give vent to his anger.

"You were drunk," the older man said bitterly; "filthy, dirty drunk and sprawled in the hay. If it hadn't been for Teel and Fallon we'd have lost everything last night, and no fault of yours that we didn't."

"What happened?"

Joshua Teel had told the story, and he had told it in concise and often profane terms. Joshua Teel was no storyteller, but starkly told, the happenings of the night were clear to everyone.

"What I want to know," Damon asked, "is where you got the whiskey. Brennan didn't sell it to you."

"None o' your damn business!"

Damon's face went white. "Don't you speak to me like that!" He came from behind the counter. "You've been behaving like a young tough long enough. You will take that pistol off and you will leave it here in the store. And you will get up in the morning—every morning—and help me here."

"I ain't a-gonna do it!" Al shouted. "I ain't no kid! I'll do what I damn' well please!"

He walked out of the store and stopped on the walk. He could hear the ring of Blane's hammer on the anvil over at the blacksmith shop, and he started in that direction. Then he stopped. Blane was worse than his pa. No use trying to talk to him.

There were still some silver dollars in his pocket, and he started for the saloon. Then he hesitated . . . Fallon would be there. About this time he usually ate breakfast, and Al did not want to see Fallon. Not this morning.

Fallon was a hero, a big man. He had saved their stock—or made out like he had. What was there to that? Just driving the cattle up out of the wash.

Al Damon stood there on the street, and his head

ached. He dreaded seeing his mother, so going to the house was out of the question. And he didn't even have a horse.

The enormity of that struck him hard. Without a horse, he could not get to see Bellows. Without a horse, he couldn't go anywhere, do anything! And how could he explain to Bellows that he, who aspired to be a member of an outlaw gang, had his horse taken from him like any brat of a kid?

He walked slowly down the street and, looking toward the flat, he glimpsed a rider moving along the wash. It was Fallon. There was no other horse like that around.

Al Damon turned quickly and went up the street to the Yankee Saloon. Brennan was standing behind the bar smoking his morning cigar.

"How's for some coffee?" Al Damon said. "And maybe a couple of them eggs?"

Brennan turned, picked up the pot, and filled a cup. "No eggs," he said, sliding the cup across the bar. "Too hard to come by."

Al Damon was about to make an angry reply, but he kept his mouth shut. He had a feeling that whatever he might say would be ignored by Brennan.

After a moment he spoke. "They fired me," he said, "just because I had a couple of drinks. Hell, I didn't do nothin'."

Brennan took the cigar from his mouth and looked thoughtfully at the ash. It was building evenly and well. He put the cigar back in his mouth and looked down the street toward the flat.

"All over nothin'," Al Damon complained. "Those cattle were all right. That ol' dam won't hold water, nohow."

Brennan took his cup and went over to the coffee pot to fill it. Fallon should be back soon, and he was looking forward to it.

Fallon puzzled him. What kind of a man was he? The events of the previous night had told him nothing he had not known. That Fallon had nerve and that he would come through when the going was rough—that he had taken for granted. What interested Brennan was what kind of a man he was otherwise. Macon Fallon was a man who held his own thoughts, expressing them rarely and to few men.

"That Fallon," Al Damon said, "he makes me tired!"

Brennan took the cigar from his mouth again, this time quickly, angrily. The ash fell off and he swore, staring down at it.

"He wears that gun around," Al Damon went on, "not even a notch on it. Not one!"

Brennan's anger stirred him to speak. It irritated him that he did speak, for he did not want to. A saloon wasn't the same as any place else. In a saloon a man was entitled to speak his mind, as long as it didn't offend anybody, and if it did, then the speaker was answerable for it. But a saloon was a place for a man to come with his troubles, and a bartender made a habit of listening without really paying much attention, unless the speaker was a friend.

Now Brennan spoke. "Nobody but a tin-horn would file a notch on his gun!" he said. "That's a kid's trick!"

"Like hell!" Al said. "Tandy Herren does it! He's got sixteen notches on his gun!"

Brennan tasted his coffee. It was too weak. He put the cup down and picked up his cigar. Suddenly, he was worried. He glanced quickly at Al, then away. How much of a fool was Al Damon?

"I doubt it," he said. "Tandy's a good hand with a gun, all right, but he'd never carve notches on his gun."

"A lot you know!" Al Damon scoffed. "I seen it!"

Instantly, he knew he had said too much. He hastily gulped the rest of his coffee. "Got to see Pa!" he said, and went out.

Sunlight was bright in the street, and for a moment he stood still, thinking of what he had said. Brennan would likely think he had seen Tandy Herren coming west. After all, what did Brennan know about where he had been or who he had seen?

He walked down the street, knowing he must make peace with his father, but reluctant to begin it. He would see his mother first. And then he would have to study out a way to get hold of a horse.

Macon Fallon rode slowly along the rim of the wash. He was still tired, but the warm sunlight felt good, and the air was fresh and clean. Moreover, he had water. A lot had gone over the dam, of course, but after the flash flood had ended, he still had a lot of water backed up in the wash.

It lapped within a few inches of the top of the dam and extended back up the wash for several hundred yards. The sun would evaporate a good bit of it, but even so, this water, with what the rain had done, would get their crops started. Several acres of corn had been planted, and a few rows of onions, potatoes, carrots, and such-like.

Turning in the saddle, he looked up toward the town. It was fresh and attractive in the morning sunlight, and certainly the setting was splendid. The mountains towered above and behind the town, giving the place an almost picture-book setting. With some management, it could become a most attractive place.

Not that it mattered in the long run. All he wanted was one good prospect on whom he could unload the claims.

The passing of time, however, worried him, for with each succeeding day the chances of someone showing up who knew the town as Buell's Bluff became greater. Or the chances of someone coming to town from Seven Pines.

Riding along the bank of the wash had brought him close to the grazing cattle. He turned toward the mountains to avoid coming close to Jim Blane, but the boy swung his horse around and cantered over to him.

"Pa told me what you did last night," Jim said. "You might have been killed."

"A man takes his chances."

"None of that stock was yours," Jim said. "It was different with Teel. He had a lot to lose."

"I couldn't have done anything without him," Fallon said. "He's quite a man, Teel is."

They talked for a few minutes about the stock, the grazing, and the water, and then Fallon rode on into the hills. He went north, and soon found himself picking his way up the slope. It was in his mind that he might find a deer, and he had not ridden this way before. He was looking for sign when he found the remains of the fire.

Night or day, a man might ride very close to that little hollow without seeing it, and any fire would have been invisible. Whatever tracks there might have been had been wiped out by the rain . . . or had they?

He stepped down from the saddle and stirred the remains of the fire. Rain had pounded the ashes into a mass, but the charred sticks were plain enough. Squatting on his heels, he moved a few of them. There was sand and ash beneath them, and beneath that, more ash and a few sticks that had not burned. Dirt had been kicked over the fire once, and then another fire had been built on top of it.

Somebody had come here, more than once . . . why? There was no water nearby, no grazing for horses within half a mile, except for the sparse brush. Altogether, it was an unlikely place for a camp, except that it offered concealment.

Mounting the black horse, Fallon found a way out of the hollow, and he had gone only a short distance when he came on the same trail Al Damon had discovered.

Fallon, wiser in these things than Al Damon, recognized it for what it was, an ancient Indian trail. It undoubtedly had also been used by game, but it had been made by Indians.

It was not much over six inches wide, for Indians habitually walk with one foot placed ahead of the other and their trails are narrow. If Indians had made it, it led to something . . . probably to water or to some source of food.

He lost the trail, found it again, and then as he walked his horse under a great leaning slab of rock he saw the track. A horse had stepped under the shadow of the leaning rock where the earth had been sheltered from rain and wind.

When he had gone a little farther his eye caught something glinting in the sun. When he reached it, he saw that it was a whiskey bottle.

Al Damon had been drunk. And he had not had the

whiskey from Brennan, who did not sell by the bottle, anyway.

Had it been Al Damon who met with somebody back there at the hollow? Or had he merely stumbled on the place as Fallon had? Yet what reason could Damon have for being here? His job had been to watch the stock.

Turning his horse back, Fallon sought out the continuation of the trail. He followed it by guess, by hunch, by a sort of instinct for such things, as much as he did by what he saw on the ground. An Indian rarely walked right out on a ridge; he usually followed the contour of a hill, and habitually sought the easiest going.

When Fallon had ridden for half an hour he realized that he was getting deeper and deeper into the mountains.

He had ventured into a gigantic cleft, invisible from the flat below, or even from the hollow where he had discovered the remains of the fire. A shoulder of the mountain presented a false wall and he had ridden behind this. The sides of the cleft sloped back steeply, ragged with projecting crags and spurs.

It was very hot, and the air was still. He was climbing steadily. Twice he drew up, studying the hills around, giving the black horse a breather. As he left one zone behind and entered another the growth was changing. The higher slopes were dotted with piñon pine, and the growth was thicker there.

He knew he should start back, but the lure of the trail led him on. There was always another bend, always another projecting rock around which he wished to see. Suddenly the trail dipped sharply, and went into a narrow cleft where the bottom was in the shadow of the towering cliffs above. The air was amazingly cool, and he smelled water.

When he found it, he saw that the water lay in a tank, a natural stone formation some fifty feet across and deep in the shadow where the sun could never reach it. A trickle of water flowed from the tank and lost itself among some rocks off to one side. There were sheep tracks a-plenty, but no tracks of horse, cow, or man.

Yet on the wall above there was Indian writing. He studied it curiously, wondering what it was meant to say. Perhaps it was an invocation to the gods of the hunt.

He watered the black, then rode on through the cleft until it suddenly dipped around and down into a great open park of grassland. This park was all of two miles wide, and perhaps three miles long. A small stream ran down the center. All around the great bowl, the mountains towered at least fifteen hundred feet, but to the north there seemed to be a gap, and that gap could very well be the canyon that ran past the town of Red Horse.

Suddenly a marmot scrabbled in the gravel on the slope, and Fallon turned his head sharply, his hand going automatically to his gun. He saw the little animal, and saw it vanish among the rocks.

He was about to start on when suddenly he saw that the trail he had been following branched here, and the left-hand branch, which he would not even have noticed had it not been for the marmot, went up, up, up among the great crags that rimmed the valley.

Only a small section of the ancient trail was visible, and it might have seemed a patch that was naturally bare, but his eye followed the hint the marmot had given and he saw there was a break in the rock.

Dismounting, he took his rifle and, scrambling over

the rocks, reached the place he sought. There was a trail, and a trail a horse could climb. He looked up, drawn by the lure of the unknown trail, drawn as he had always been. But the hour was late and he was far from town.

Descending into the open space, he started across the grassland and, when he was near the stream, a deer suddenly started from the grass. He lifted his rifle, catching a quick sight of the back of the neck just above the shoulders. He squeezed off his shot, and the deer fell.

When he had butchered it, he started for the break in the hills which he was sure was the canyon leading toward home.

Suddenly a rider appeared, riding up from some hollow where he had remained hidden until now. And then another appeared, and another and another. And then another rider appeared, far on his right, and there were five, six riders there.

Utes. . . .

Macon Fallon touched the black horse on the shoulder. "Ready, boy . . . we may have to run again."

He held his rifle in his right hand and he rode forward, seeming to look neither to the right nor to the left, head up, the butt of the rifle on his thigh. Wind stirred the grass, and he looked ahead to the opening of the canyon.

How far? Half a mile? A mile? Distance was deceiving on these hot, still afternoons. The wind stirred again, faintly, like a living thing awakening from a long sleep.

The riders were drawing nearer. "All right, boy," Fallon said quietly, and the black horse began to lope. It was an easy, space-eating lope, and he was riding toward the point of a triangle, of which the lines of Indians made the two sides.

His mouth was dry, and when he touched his tongue to his lips they, too, seemed dry.

They were closer . . . within rifle-shot soon. The black had come a long way, but the horse was good for the run to the canyon.

How far now? He had gained a few hundred yards, perhaps as much as a quarter of a mile.

"All right, boy . . . *now!*"

With a bound the black horse was off, running as if it was shot. Before him the canyon gaped. Suddenly the Indians had begun to whoop, and they were coming on, running hard.

The nearest one was over-anxious . . . he fired, and the sound of the shot racketed against the cliffs. The black was running fine, and the way was clear. But they were pulling up on him now, cutting across to head him off. He glanced to right and left. The nearest ones were close . . . too close.

The canyon opened before him, then closed to scarcely twenty yards wide. There were boulders and broken slabs of rock on the left, and Fallon eased the racing horse.

"We'll make our stand, boy," he said, and wheeled the horse into the shelter of the boulders and hit the ground running.

The nearest Indian was no more than fifty feet behind and raced on past. Macon Fallon swung with his rifle and shot into the horse that carried the second Indian. Then, pivoting on his right heel, he fired at the Indian that had gone on past and was now turning.

He jacked a shell into the chamber and waited.

It was cool here in the shadow of the giant cliffs. Only a streamer of sky showed above him. The sand was still hard-packed from the swift waters that had so recently run over it. It would be night soon.

He glanced back again—the Indian pony stood off to one side. The Ute lay sprawled, the sand darkened and enriched by his blood.

Out in front the valley was empty; only the long grass stirred in the wind.

CHAPTER 4

T HAT WAS THE night the big train came to Red Horse.

They came in the late afternoon, forty-two wagons, streaming down the long hill, rumbling across the bridge.

Brennan heard them coming, and looked out his window and down the street toward the bridge. The biggest wagon train he had ever seen, and Macon Fallon nowhere around.

He called his Negro from the still. "Leave that for now," he said urgently. "Go get Josh Teel."

Al Damon was in the store. "All right . . . pay him," he told his father. "I figure there should be an election. I figure we should vote, get us a marshal with a badge, and we should have us a mayor."

"The boy's right," Blane said. "I don't hold with violence, and Fallon has shown himself a violent man. Sure, he saved our stock, but that gives him no right to hold us up for thirty percent of what we make."

"We'd better talk to the others. We'll call a meeting. There's Hamilton, Budge, Teel—"

"You can count him out. He'll stand with Fallon."

The wagons came up the street, the big white-topped wagons, drawn by great teams of bulls, the heavy wagons with sunbonneted women and roughly dressed men, men in galluses and boots, men with rifles and men with belt guns, men ready to trade, and some looking to settle. They flooded into the stores, and for the time being all thought of Fallon was dropped.

Joshua Teel came in and had a drink with Brennan. He had a cold beer, for Brennan had found an ice cave in the lava flow at the upper end of town.

"Ain't seen him," Teel said. "He cut out right after sunup to have a look at the water. Young Blane said he stopped by the herd, then cut up into the hills."

Brennan was worried.

He watched the wagons roll up the street. He watched the men get down, and some of them walked up to the saloon. He served them drinks and listened, and they asked about the prospects.

"Have to see Fallon," Brennan said. "It's his town."

A big, square-faced man looked up belligerently. "I never heard of no man who could run the town I'm in," he said. "Who is this Fallon?"

"He's a good man," Brennan replied. "He started the town."

"All right, he started it. So where is he?"

"He'll be around."

Al Damon had come in. He still carried a few of the silver dollars. He put one of them on the bar and said, "Fallon ain't gonna run this town forever. We're goin' to have an election. We'll vote us a marshal and a mayor."

Brennan ignored him, but he felt a little shock of doubt. If an election was called, there was no question of it being called to help Fallon in any way. It could only be called to be rid of him.

He worked swiftly and silently, talking little, and then

only to reply to questions, but he was aware that Al Damon was doing some talking, and none of it friendly to Fallon.

With the rush of business, he stayed open until ten, and the saloon was orderly. Only the big man, whose name was Gleason, showed any inclination to trouble.

The wagon train had started out from Ft. Leaven-worth to come to the Nevada and California mines. They would rest and recuperate here for two or three days, then go on west.

Wagon trains were few these days, for the time of the gold rush was long past. Nowadays the wagon trains were likely to be freighters, carrying cargo to the mines or ore from them. In this train there should be a number of men or families who might be useful to Red Horse.

Fallon should be here. It had always been Fallon who sorted the men out, who looked for strong, competent men with trades, men who wanted to do something and create something. There was no one to do that now. And it was unlike Fallon to be gone.

Teel dropped in just before closing. He was gloomy. "I don't like it, John. There's a lot of talk around about electing a mayor and appointing a marshal. Al Damon's doing most of the talking, but young Jim Blane is, too."

"Where is Fallon?" Brennan said anxiously. "If ever, he should be here now."

Half an hour before closing time Luther Semple rode slowly into Red Horse. From a nearby bluff he had watched the wagon train and had decided that now, among all this crowd of strangers, he would have a good chance to take stock of the town.

The wagon train was such a big one that attacking the town while it was there was simply out of the question.

There must be a hundred men, he thought, or close to it, with that train. Until now, they had been trusting to the reports of Al Damon, but Semple did not place any confidence in his reports. It was obvious that Al did not like Fallon, and he might have underestimated him.

Lute Semple was not particularly bright, but he had an animal instinct for danger and he had been one of those at the wagon the night Fallon rode up on them. He had not seen him, but he had heard that voice.

Since then, Al had described Fallon so it would be hard to miss him. Lute Semple wanted to see Fallon, to estimate the danger involved; for Lute had survived a good deal longer than many of his comrades because he had no desire to make a reputation, nor any urge to face a dangerous man in any kind of a gun battle.

Semple rode into Red Horse unnoticed in the confusion following the arrival of the wagon train, almost half of which was made up of freight wagons. The teamsters were well-armed and competent-looking men. There were about thirty of them, tough men and veterans of many an Indian fight.

Semple tied his horse a few doors down from the Yankee Saloon, then after a careful look around, he entered the saloon and ordered a drink.

The first person he recognized was John Brennan himself, and he remembered him from both Abilene and Corinne. Taking his drink, Lute Semple found his way to a table in the corner and sat down.

Had Brennan recognized him? He thought not. In any event, Brennan would have no reason to suspect him of anything, for Brennan had never, so far as Semple was aware, known anything about him.

A lot of money was being spent. Semple could see the

teamsters crowding to the bar, and the whiskey they bought was surprisingly good.

Fallon did not seem to be anywhere around, and that worried him. If he was not here, where was he?

Semple was sitting at the table when Joshua Teel entered. He had never seen Teel before, but he recognized the type. Oddly enough, Teel had been born in a log cabin not three-quarters of a mile from Semple's home.

After he finished his whiskey, Semple got up and left quietly. John Brennan, recorking a bottle, turned his eyes to watch him go. Luther Semple had not counted on Brennan's good memory, or his interest in his customers.

"Teel," Brennan said, leaning on the bar, "you ever hear of Luther Semple?"

"Semple? There were some Semples back home. The ones I knew of were a no-good outfit . . . though probably were others who were good folks. . . . Why?"

"Lute Semple just walked out of here, and I'd make a small bet he's with Bellows. A few years back there were a lot of murders over on the Republican—buffalo-skinners murdered in camp . . . shot in the back. The camps were robbed, and at first it was laid to Indians, but then it was figured to be a well-organized gang.

"Semple was around about that time, and a man he traveled with was caught with a rifle stolen off a murdered man. Semple disappeared—dropped clean out of sight.

"Later, he was around Corinne. Back in those days it was a booming town on the Lake. If you see him around, keep an eye on him."

Joshua Teel left by the back door and cut around between the buildings. He stood in the shadows and surveyed the street with care. He saw Semple almost at once, a tall, slightly stooped man with drooping mustaches, a man who stood alone on the street, or bent to peer into the windows of the closed shops.

Stepping out from the buildings, Teel loafed along in the shadows. He noted the horse tied at the hitch rail, a tall, clean-limbed bay with a rifle in the scabbard.

It was after midnight when Semple mounted up and rode out of town. Listening, Teel heard no drum of hoofs on the bridge. Semple had gone down on the flat, then. Teel returned to his own place and turned in.

———

MACON FALLON HAD found shelter for his horse among the boulders. Outside the canyon mouth there was no movement. His horse had drunk, and was cropping at some grass growing in the space between some of the higher boulders. Fallon settled himself down for a long stay, and waited for the sun to go down.

Could the Utes get around behind him in any way? It was possible. His only way out was down the canyon toward Red Horse, for they blocked the opening before him. Yet suppose there was a way down from the cliffs above? Supposing even two or three could circle around, slip down the cliff, and lie in wait for him?

The sun declined, seemed to hesitate, then vanished. It was twilight within the canyon now, although still bright out on the basin.

The Utes knew that when darkness came he would ride away down the canyon to safety, yet they made no further attempt to push the attack. That meant they were either waiting for darkness to attack—which not many Indians liked to do—or they had gotten around behind him and were not worried.

Suddenly, the black horse's head came up. His head up, ears pricked, he looked off down the canyon. Something was down there, behind him.

Carefully, Fallon replaced the fired cartridges in his Winchester, and waited. When darkness came, he took a last drink at the water, then mounted up. Slipping the Winchester into the scabbard, he drew his .44 pistol.

Riding out quietly from the boulders, he turned his horse back toward the valley from which he had come. This, he hoped, they would not expect, for he would be riding away from safety.

The sand made little sound as he walked the horse along. The end of the canyon was like a gigantic door . . . beyond was the valley, the star-lit skies. He had ridden sixty yards out of the canyon mouth before they discovered him.

He smelled smoke, and at the same time he saw an Indian rear up from the ground and start toward him. Deliberately, he dropped the muzzle of his gun on the slim dark figures, and fired.

He saw the jerk of the Indian's body as the bullet struck, and at the same moment he touched the black with the spurs and was off, riding at a dead run into the wide-open spaces of the valley.

Could he find the other trail? At night it would look different, but long ago he had cultivated the habit of all wise travelers in wild country, of turning to look back. Faced from the opposite direction, a trail can look vastly different, and if compelled to retrace one's trail such a precaution is essential.

He rode at a dead run for a quarter of a mile or so, then slowed and turned at right angles, making for the valley's eastern side. He found the gap, started toward it, then recalled the steep trail, and mounted to the top of the cliffs above the valley.

Leaning forward, he peered above to his right, searching for the notch in the rock, and hoping he could choose the right one.

Here, in the still, cool night, he could smell the dusty grass and the sage. Behind him there would be pursuit, and they would be sure he had come toward this trail, which he knew.

Fallon spoke softly to his horse. That horse was working overtime keeping him out of trouble—keeping him alive, even; for a man without a horse in this country was often as good as a dead man . . . that was the reason for hanging horse thieves.

Fallon rode carefully, easing toward the trail he had come over that afternoon. Suddenly, when almost past it, he saw what he believed was the notch he wanted. Turning abruptly, he put his horse up the steep slope. Instinctively, it held to the trail.

They climbed steeply, winding around boulders, and, suddenly emerging at the top, he was among the pines. He sought a place among the trees and boulders not far from the trail up which he climbed, and there he settled down for the night.

He slept fitfully, allowing the black horse to keep watch. With the dawn he was awake, listening. But he heard no sound but the wind in the pines, the lazy cropping of his horse. He sat still for some time, testing the morning with all his senses. If Indians were about, he wanted to know it. While he waited, he ate some pine nuts undiscovered by the birds.

After a while he got to his feet, saddled the horse, and led it to the trail. He studied the ground with care and found no tracks or sign of any kind save that of his own horse. Nevertheless, he hesitated to descend into what might well be a trap. So far as he was aware, only two routes of escape were possible to him, and perhaps the Indians knew it, too. They might be waiting somewhere below.

Mounting, he turned away from the trail by which he had reached the crest of the mountain, and rode along the slope under the pines, his rifle ready for any eventuality.

The morning was clear and bright, the air fresh and pleasantly cool. His horse trod on pine needles, and pines were all about him.

He followed a game trail along the slope. Occasionally, through a break in the pines he could see in front of him, off to the left, a towering dome of a mountain. It had a distinctive shape and looked to be the highest anywhere around.

Suddenly the slope seemed to drop completely away, and he found himself on the verge of a tremendous declivity where the mountain fell away some four thousand feet to the valley below. This must be, had to be, the Big Smoky Valley.

A few minutes later he found a spring trickling from the rocks. Here he drank, and allowed his horse to drink.

The rocks around the spring were broken and jagged, a wide vein of quartz intruding the sedimentary rock. As he knelt to drink again he glimpsed tiny, gleaming fragments on the sand at the bottom.

Gold? It could be . . . or fool's gold. He scooped some of the sand from the bottom of the catch basin and, spreading it out, managed with a wet twig to isolate several small flakes and grains.

The shade of trees bending over the spring seemed not to affect the gleam of the particles. He tested several flakes with a knife blade, and found they could be cut.

His guess was that they were gold. He had worked as a miner, but had had little to do with gold except as money. Several mines in which he had worked had no visible gold before the ore was milled.

If this was gold, he might get enough at the bottom of the small falls farther down the slope to salt one of his claims; but to return here would mean risking another run-in with the Utes. While he stayed there in the shade beside the spring, he washed out a tiny stack of gold, which he carefully put away in an old envelope he'd been carrying in his coat pocket.

Returning, he decided, was unnecessary. It was far easier to salt a claim with imagination than with gold. After all, it was what a man imagined he would get from a claim that sold him, not what he actually saw. Often it was easier to sell a man a worthless hole in the ground than a good prospect.

He was hungry, for he had eaten nothing since breakfast of the previous day, except for an occasional handful of pine nuts. But he had no food and he hesitated to fire a shot for fear it would bring the Utes around him. It was not the first time he had been hungry, and he had long ago learned that grumbling about what can't be helped did no good at all. Remounting his horse, he worked his way farther along the slope. The dome he had seen was off to the northwest and, as near as he could judge, not more than four miles away.

He was high up . . . judging by the plant growth around him, he was upwards of ten thousand feet. He had gone but a short distance toward the dome when the ground fell steeply away into a magnificent gorge, wild and lonely. His eyes followed it toward the northwest.

This could be the gorge he had started up when leaving the hollow by the old Indian trail, and had veered off to the south. If it was that gorge, he was well on his way home—if he could only get down to the bottom of the canyon. But nowhere did there seem to be a route by which he could descend. He was trapped on an island in the sky, not over three miles long and about half a mile wide.

He turned his horse and rode southwest again, back toward the Indians. On the east this plateau fell steeply away for a thousand feet or more, and then there was another steep descent, not quite so abrupt, to the bottom of Smoky Valley.

Finally, after hours of searching, he found a way off the top, and went over the rim, the black horse almost sliding on his haunches. After going down several hundred feet, accompanied by cascades of sand and gravel, he found a game trail. After a mile it began a descent to the bottom of the canyon, and he followed it down.

He had been on the mountain the whole day, and when he reached the bottom it was dark.

Knowing enough of such canyons, he made no attempt to go farther, but found a bench beside the stream and made camp. The bottoms of such canyons were littered with boulders, fallen logs, debris of all kinds, and there were, as well, sudden falls that might drop off for fifty feet or more. Usually, if one could find it, there would be an Indian trail or a game trail skirting the edge of the creek. This would show him the way around any falls there might be.

At noon the following day, Fallon rode up the street of

Red Horse, a Red Horse such as he had never seen. The street was crowded with wagons and with strangers. Suddenly he saw Blane and started toward him. Blane looked up, saw him coming, and abruptly turned away and went inside, closing the door behind him.

Surprised, Fallon rode on up the street. A new saloon had opened and above a door near the saloon was a sign: OFFICE OF THE MAYOR.

Brennan watched him tie his horse and came out on the street. "You played hell," he said. "Where've you been?"

Briefly, Fallon explained.

"Last night," Brennan said, "they had an election. It was Blane and Damon behind it, and Al talking it up all over town. The way I figure, Blane expected to be mayor . . . well, he didn't get to even have a look-in. This newcomer, he had the votes from the wagon train, and he was elected. Not only that, but he appointed himself a marshal and a deputy marshal."

Fallon looked at Brennan unbelievingly.

"That's right," Brennan said, "a marshal and a deputy, and if I ever looked on a troublemaker, it's that Gleason. He's big and he's mean, and he's been asking around for you."

"I'll be here."

"Fallon," Brennan said, "go easy. There's at least sixty men here now who weren't here when you left, and those men only know that you're supposed to own the town. They don't accept that—not for a minute, they don't. The rest of them accepted it because they figured they owed you something. This bunch don't figure they owe you anything."

Macon Fallon looked down the street, anger stirring within him. This was *his* town. He had started it, he had cleaned up the street, he had . . . But what was he kicking about? After all, he only wanted to sell a couple of claims and get out.

"Maybe it will all work out for the best," he said. "We'll see."

Brennan was surprised at Fallon's words. He was not sure what he had expected, but it was not this.

Fallon went into the saloon and drank coffee until Brennan brought him a meal. As he sat there he did some serious thinking.

Later, alone in his upstairs apartment, he wrote three letters. He had just completed them when there was a rap on his door. It was Joboy, Brennan's Negro handyman.

"Boss says there's somebody downstairs to see you all." Joboy hesitated. "It's that mayor fella and the marshal."

Fallon got to his feet. Carefully, he put on his black coat. But first he checked his gun.

"Mr. Fallon," he said, looking at himself in the cracked mirror, "luck!" And then he added, "You may need it."

As soon as he reached the head of the stairs, he could see he was in for trouble. The bar was lined with men, all strangers.

"Joboy," he said over his shoulder to the Negro, "tell Josh Teel I want to see him."

Joboy chuckled. "Mistah Fallon, you don't need to tell that man. He's already down at the end of the bar—with a shotgun!"

Glancing over the room then, Fallon saw at a separate table Riordan, Shelley, and Zeno Yearly. A yard or so away, seated alone, but with his back to a corner, was Devol.

Fallon suddenly felt good. It had been a long time since he had had friends. A wandering man loses much, and nowhere had Fallon sunk roots, nowhere had he remained long enough to know people. Several of these men were family men, with responsibilities to their families, yet they were here.

Coolly, he walked down the steps, and as he reached the bottom, with all eyes on him, Devol got to his feet.

"Your table, Mr. Fallon," he said quietly, and then under his breath he said, "We're with you—all the way."

"Thanks," Fallon said, and drew back a chair.

He had not looked at anyone after that first glance from the head of the stairs. Nor would he. If they wished to talk to him, they could come to him.

Brennan, with a fine flourish, brought a bottle of wine to his table, wiped the table with care, and put down the wine and a glass. He spoke quietly. "The big fellow in the plaid shirt—that's Gleason. His deputy is the man in the black hat, over by the door."

"And the mayor?"

"Here he comes. . . ."

Brennan filled the wine glass two-thirds full, then put down the bottle and went back to his bar.

A shadow fell across the table as the man stepped between Fallon and the light.

Yes, Macon Fallon was feeling good. He had evaded the Utes with a whole skin. He had come back to town. He had good, solid men behind him, and a glass of wine before him.

He lifted the glass.

"You're Fallon?" said the man standing there.

"I am Macon Fallon." He continued to look at the play of light in the wine. "You wished to speak to me? If it is about arrangements to occupy buildings in the town, you may speak to Mr. Brennan, at the bar. He is my agent in such matters."

"I am afraid you don't understand the situation, Fallon." The voice was cold. "We don't intend to pay any rent, or any percentage, either. We've moved in, and we plan to stay."

Fallon leaned back in his chair, tasting the wine. "Excellent vintage," he said. "Brennan is to be complimented."

He looked up . . . it was fortunate that he was a poker player, for he looked right into the eyes of Iron John Buell, swindler, card shark, and gunman. He was all of that and more. He was the original founder of Buell's Bluff.

Macon Fallon, who had played his part in many peculiar scenes in his life, turned not a hair, nor betrayed by even a flicker of an eyelash that he recognized Iron John.

He took his time, holding the advantage he wanted. Iron John was standing as though awaiting his decision, and every moment he stood there was an added advantage for Fallon.

Fallon tasted the wine again, and then carefully he put down his glass. "You were saying?" he asked.

"I said"—Buell's voice was loud—"we don't intend to pay any rent, or any percentage, either. We don't figure you own this town."

"I see," Fallon smiled slightly. "I expect you will be moving on, then, you and your friends. Although," and he spoke loud enough to be heard clearly, "we welcome citizens with trades who are willing to abide by the rules laid down."

He sipped his wine. "Of course," he said, "you cannot expect anyone to abide by your trumped-up election. Not more than half a dozen of the men in this room are entitled to vote. The others have not established residence.

"Moreover," he added, "as in the case of most mining communities, the first settlers draw up the rules of the community, and such rules are accepted in law. I have those rules. Your election was apparently held in ignorance or defiance of them. That is scarcely the right attitude."

He put down his glass. He felt very cool, very sure of himself. This was Iron John Buell who stood here, a very tough man and a worse crook than he, Macon Fallon, could ever attempt to be.

"It has come to my attention," he said quietly, but his voice could be heard in every corner of the room, "that you have appointed a marshal, and even a *deputy* marshal. We have had no trouble here, and we expect none . . . unless it be from Utes or from the Bellows gang."

Iron John Buell was uneasy. He had expected nothing like this. Macon Fallon was altogether too sure of himself . . . why?

He was losing face, he was suddenly sure of that. Without thinking, he said, "Marshal . . . arrest this man!"

Fallon smiled. "Arrest me? For what? For drinking wine? For minding my own affairs?"

Gleason was pleased. There had been altogether too much talk. He stepped around Buell and up to the table.

"You!" he said loudly. *"Get up!"*

He dropped a large hand to Fallon's shoulder, and Macon Fallon, who had never liked to be touched, brushed the hand away, and at the same instant he jerked hard on the toe he had hooked around Gleason's leg.

Off balance, Gleason's arms pawed at the air, and then he fell. He hit the floor hard, and before he could stir a shotgun muzzle was put against his throat by Shelley, who had not risen from the table.

Gleason's flailing arms eased back to the floor and he lay still, his face a sickly yellow, for which Macon Fallon, an understanding man, blamed him not at all. A shotgun against the throat is a very persuasive argument.

Fallon lifted his wine glass again. "One thing I think I should explain," he said in the same quiet voice, heard by all, "the dam which holds back water for irrigation was built by me, with some help from Mr. Teel. The rights to that water are in my hands. Furthermore, the only source of water for the town is the spring on this property, which belongs to me. I will allow traveling water—once only—to anyone wishing to move on across the desert. To all those who refuse to pay their rent or percentage, I shall allow nothing at all as long as they remain here."

"You can't get away with this!" Buell protested angrily. "I am the mayor!"

"On the contrary," Fallon replied, "I am acting mayor. No legal elections have been held by bona fide residents of the town."

He got to his feet. "Let me say this. I arrived here first. I cleaned up the street, retouched the signs, built the dam, helped to plant the first crops. I assigned the businesses and places of business. I put Red Horse on the map!"

He paused, then looked right at Buell. "If there is anyone present who can claim to have been here before me, and who can justly claim the site was not abandoned, he has only to speak up now."

Iron John Buell felt a sinking in his stomach. This man Fallon knew him . . . Fallon knew who he was, what he had done.

Buell felt like a fool. Fallon turned aside. "Joboy, will you fill three canteens for me? And bring them here."

"What's that for?" Buell demanded.

"For you, Mr. Buell"—Fallon's voice was suddenly harsh—"and for your high-binding marshal and deputy marshal. You get three canteens of water . . . and this warning: *Get out and stay out!*"

Buell started to bluster. He hoped somebody behind him would say something, but the men at the bar were silent. He glanced around desperately. Gleason lay upon the floor, the shotgun still at his throat, and the man who held the shotgun sat at the table with others who probably also backed Fallon.

Abruptly, he turned and started for the door.

"*Buell!*" Fallon's voice rang in the room, and Iron John almost cringed. "You forgot your canteen."

He turned to the table beside him. "Shelley, will you and Teel escort these men to their horses? And Riordan, would you accompany them, please?"

Buell hesitated. "You sending us out *tonight?*"

Macon Fallon nodded. "Not only tonight. I am sending you out right now . . . this minute. If you travel at night your water will last longer; and may I say, you'd better waste no time if you expect it to last until you get to a water hole."

When they had gone, Fallon stepped up to the bar. The men who stood there were mostly good men, he thought, as he glanced along the bar. He said, "John, the drinks are on me. Serve these gentlemen, will you?"

Then he spoke more quietly. "Gentlemen, I quite understand how exorbitant my demands must seem, but when the town has been put into some sort of shape, the amount will be cut—cut quite liberally. We need good men here. Now, if any of you wish to remain you may talk to Mr. Brennan or, in the morning, to me."

He turned away and went up the stairs.

When he had closed the door behind him he stood still, soaked with perspiration. His collar felt tight, his coat was hot. He peeled off the coat and sat down astride a chair, his arms leaning on the back.

He still could not believe he had won.

———

GINIA BLANE WAS sewing, but she was also listening. The story of the events at the Yankee Saloon had swept the town, and her father could not believe it. Neither could Damon, and they had been talking it over since breakfast.

Her father had been one of the leaders in the move to oust Fallon from control of the town, and Damon had been with him all the way. For the first time since she could remember, Al and his father had agreed about something. There had been others, of course. That her father had expected to be chosen as Mayor she knew, and she also knew what a shock it had been when the newcomers had deliberately shunted him aside.

Ginia Blane knew nothing of politics, but she had sense enough to recognize organization; and when Buell had been nominated the seconding of the motion had come too quickly—obviously the motion and its second-ing had been agreed upon beforehand.

Budge had then been nominated, a man with no chance for election, and then a motion had come to move the nominations be closed and that was promptly seconded. Buell's election had been a foregone conclusion.

Her father still did not know what had happened to him, but he had been rudely shocked by the manner in which he had been shunted aside, and he could not be-lieve they had failed, even then, to cope with Fallon.

Her father could not face Fallon, and she did not blame him for that.

Al Damon was there also, and he moved his leg, now easing the position of the gun he wore. Al, Ginia de-cided, was afraid somebody would not realize that he was wearing a gun. Al was puzzled.

"But what did he *do?*" he demanded. "You say he just sat there. He must have done *something.*"

Needham was telling about it, and he was enjoying it. "I tell you he didn't *do* anything!" He chuckled. "Why, you'd of thought he was the schoolmaster and that there Buell a young boy brought up for discipline. He made Buell look like a fool; and then of course, he told him about the water."

"The water?"

"That he owned it. That he would shut off anybody who didn't want to pay up. He did say he'd give traveling water to anybody who wanted to leave."

Ginia thought . . . of course, of course, why didn't I realize that? Without water, nobody can live, and the water is his.

"A man could slip down at night and get water from

back of the dam," Damon suggested. "He couldn't watch all of that."

"That water?" Mrs. Damon sniffed. "I wouldn't drink it . . . or wash with it, if there was anything else. Cattle walk in it, drink from it—everything."

"I don't know why everybody is so anxious to be rid of him," Ginia interrupted. "What has he done? He's worked harder and done more than anybody else in town."

"I've worked as hard as anybody!" Blane protested.

"You worked very hard," Ginia agreed, "in your own shop and for your own profit. Fallon built the dam. Fallon weeded the street, trimmed the trees, repaired the boardwalks, and did a hundred little things to make the town a good place to live."

"Well, he's gettin' paid for it, too!" Damon said resentfully.

"And why not?" Ginia broke her thread, and held up the blouse she was making and studied it critically. "And when I think of what you almost did, I feel positively ill. That Gleason! Every time he looked at me I felt like taking a bath. And you all wanted a change—thank heavens, you didn't get it!"

They were silent, but unconvinced.

———

THE YANKEE SALOON was cool and still. The only sound was that made by Macon Fallon, idly shuffling a deck of cards. He built his bottom stock with care, dealt four hands, and glanced at his own.

Brennan picked up the hand nearest him as he passed the table. Four nines. He picked up the second, it was four sixes. "Not bad," he said dryly. "Are they all that good?"

"Mine is better," Fallon said, and spread four kings on the table.

Brennan put his cloth upon the end of the bar and sat down. He lighted a fresh cigar. Macon Fallon watched him, smiling a little. Brennan had something on his mind.

"Al Damon," Brennan said, taking the cigar from his lips, "was the first one I heard who talked of an election."

Macon Fallon swept the cards together, cut them, shifted the cut, and built a center stock, cut to the center and had his stock on the bottom, ready for dealing.

"You know, and I know," Brennan continued, "that it is not likely he thought of that himself. His pa may have, but Al was talking it up before I ever heard a word of it from Blane or Damon."

Macon Fallon dealt himself two aces face up, then second-dealt a third ace.

"Those silver dollars, now." Brennan drew deep on his cigar. "Damon never spends any silver money that I've seen, but that's all Al ever spends.

"I've been keeping track . . . nobody spends silver dollars but him. Silver money is scarce in camp . . . fact of the matter is, any kind of money is scarce."

"So?"

"That Bellows man . . . Lute Semple. He was in here the other night . . . he paid for his drinks with a silver dollar—mint new."

Fallon made a neat stack of the deck and put it down on the table. "Do you think Al is meeting some of the Bellows outfit?"

"He didn't get whiskey from me. He had whiskey.

There's no silver money in town except half dollars, and he has new silver dollars."

Brennan looked at the lengthening ash on his cigar. "About three months ago an Army pay wagon bound from Carson to Fort Churchill was robbed. Four men killed . . . it was laid to Indians."

Brennan looked up at Fallon. "That Army payroll was mostly in brand-new silver dollars."

Fallon looked out the doorway, watching the sunlight fall across the walk. It all tied in with the fire where somebody had been meeting—nobody would purposely camp in such a spot—and with the empty whiskey bottle he had found.

"You could be right," he said. Then he told Brennan about the fire he had found.

"What's next?" Brennan asked.

Fallon shrugged. "Wait. Look, John, Al's a kid. Sure, he's nineteen, and you and me, we were men making our way long before that, but he's nineteen like we were fourteen. Maybe he'll come to his senses."

"You know he won't," Brennan replied. "Fallon, how many times have you seen an Al Damon strap on a gun like that? First he wants to be a gunfighter; he admires outlaws and gunfighters. He straps on a gun and convinces himself he's a big man. He practices in secret. If it stopped there, that would be fine; but he's got to kill somebody.

"A man who's a gunfighter, he's killed men, and unless a fellow has, he can't have the name. He's not thinking about the fact that the other man will be shooting, too. In your dreams you never draw too slow, never get killed . . . not in daydreams, anyway. So sooner or later he's going to have to use that gun."

Fallon drew the cards to him again. Idly, he ran them through his fingers. "John, what would you have me do? Go to his father? I don't believe Al would give up the gun because his father told him to—in fact, I know he wouldn't.

"Maybe I should go to Al? You know what would happen then. He'd try to face me, and I might have to kill him. I don't want to draw a gun on that boy, John."

Brennan was silent. Of course, what Fallon said was true. When they went as far as Al Damon had gone, mighty few of them stopped before they killed or were killed. Perhaps fortunately, most of them were killed.

Fallon stacked the cards again and got up. "Going up to the claim," he said, and went out.

Irritation was riding him. He had remained too long in Red Horse. He had a few dollars now, little enough, it was true, but he would be smart to saddle up and ride out. He could get on the stage route and follow it through to Carson. He was playing the fool, staying here. His every instinct told him the top was about to blow off and he was standing right in the middle of it.

He walked up to the mine, peeled off his coat and shirt, and puttered around. In the drift he worked for a good two hours, working away with his pick at the face of the drift, working to rid himself of his worry rather than for any hope of finding anything. In fact, he had no such hope.

He could drive his pick into a crack and wedge off a good-sized chunk. It fell around his feet, and he let it fall. Finally, he put down the pick and went to the mouth of the tunnel.

Red Horse lay below him, and he looked at it with surprise. There were a dozen people on the street, two wagons, and several saddle horses. Lines of wash hung outside nearly every cabin. Three tents had gone up in a neat row back of the Damon store. Beyond the town he could see rows of bright green where corn was up and starting to leaf out . . . the weeks had gone by too fast.

Two small boys came out of the Damon store and started down the street. There ought to be a school. That was one thing the town needed . . . a school.

Well, it was none of his affair. He had made his decision as he looked down over the town. Whether or not he sold his claims, he would pull out at the end of another month. He would give it that long.

Yet even as he decided, he felt an odd sinking in his stomach. He was a fool to wait. Buell might come back. Bellows might come. Anything might happen.

He picked up his shirt and put it on and stuffed it into his pants. He was buttoning his shirt when Ginia Blane rode up on the shoulder where the claim lay.

"How do you do, Mr. Acting Mayor?" she said politely.

He glanced at her sourly. "I have no desire," he said, "to be acting mayor or any other kind."

"As much as I do not like you," Ginia confessed, "you have done a lot for the town. You deserve to be mayor."

"I don't like you, either," Fallon replied coolly, "and I deserve nothing of the kind. The only reason I interfered was because the man was so obviously a crook."

"John Buell," she said, looking straight into his eyes, "of Buell's Bluff."

He finished buttoning his shirt, giving all his attention to the buttons. She knew then. Well, that tore it. Now he was getting out of town. When he lifted his eyes to her his face betrayed nothing.

"I am afraid that I don't get a chance to do enough for the town to be a good mayor at the stage this town is now passing through. There are too many interruptions for me."

"Don't ignore the subject, Mr. Fallon. I am sure no honest man would be so adept at turning things to his advantage as you seem to be. My father is an impatient man, Mr. Fallon, but not a suspicious one. I am afraid that I am suspicious.

"You hesitated out there on the trail that day before you named the town, and then you saw our sorrel, and you came up very quickly with a name . . . Red Horse.

"Naturally, when we moved into town I was curious, and was surprised there wasn't the name of the town anywhere. There was only one sign missing—the sign in front of the bank."

"You have a devious mind, Miss Blane. When one is so suspicious of others, it makes a man wonder if there isn't something wrong with the thinking of that person."

She was attractive, too damned attractive. Suddenly he wanted to be rid of her. Why didn't she ride back down to town? Was she spying on him? Yet for what reason? She seemed to know all that was necessary to expose him.

"You know about Buell's Bluff?"

"Yes . . . I was a little girl at the time, but I had an uncle who was very excited about it until the boom collapsed." She regarded him with those cool eyes. "It was a fraud."

"Is a town ever a fraud?" he said gently. "A town is made up of people, and until there are people there can be no town. John Buell is gone. The people who came with him are gone, and I did not let them come back. So what we have here is a town not only with a new name, but with a new life." He looked up at her and smiled. "Miss Blane, how can a collection of old, empty buildings be a fraud?"

"You are very glib."

"Your father is here . . . he is part of the town. Is he a fraud? Is Joshua Teel a fraud? Or your friend Damon?"

She was not to be put off. "What about you? Are you a fraud?"

He shrugged, spreading his hands. "Who can say what he is? Are you so sure of yourself? I am not sure at all. I do not know what I am.

"Look." He swept a hand toward the town. "There it is. I think the prospect is pleasant. It was an empty shell. Now there are homes here, citizens earning a living. There are fields with crops springing up, there is water to irrigate, soon one of our cows will calve. Our town may die, but now it lives . . . let us help it."

He dropped his hands. "Anyway, what difference can one man make in the destiny of a town? If I were a fraud, need it matter? The town would go on without me."

She considered that, and then she shook her head slowly. "No, Mr. Fallon, I do not think it would. As much as I dislike you, and as much as some of them down there dislike you, I do not think the town would live or could live without you."

It was a point gained, and he grasped it quickly. "Perhaps, then," he said quietly, "I am not a fraud."

When she was safely down the hill he sat down and swore. That damned girl had a way of talking that angered him. He should keep his mouth shut and let her talk, but she kept prying, and something forced him to come up with the answers.

That the town would die without him was nonsense. But the thought irritated him, and it brought a sense of guilt that he did not appreciate. After all, what difference did it make? Was he his brother's keeper?

But that was not the problem now. If Ginia told what she knew—and there was no reason she shouldn't— there would be an exodus from the town as sudden and dramatic as that other one, years before. At all costs, he must make a deal.

CHAPTER 5

MACON FALLON RETURNED to his quarters above the saloon and put together a small pack. From Damon, in lieu of cash, he had a few days previously taken some clothing, blankets, and other necessities. Now he packed his clothing, his extra ammunition, the few toilet articles he used, and a couple of books he had found in the hotel.

Only when that was done did he go to the stable behind the saloon, where he watered the black horse, filled the manger with forage, and checked the horse's shoes to be sure he was ready for travel.

"When we go," he whispered to the black horse, "we will go fast and far . . . and it can happen at just any time."

Uneasily, he paused in the stable door. Why not saddle up and go right now? Why wait for the chance of a big killing that might never materialize? He had escaped from the Utes as much by luck as by ability, and he had outsmarted and outmaneuvered Iron John Buell only with the help of his loyal friends. He might not be so lucky again.

The Utes were out there, undoubtedly watching the town, and Bellows was out there, too. Within the town there was unrest, and at least some people who disliked him. And there was Al Damon, his gun belted on, itching for a chance to prove he was a tough man.

Sourly, Fallon looked at the town. What was wrong with him? Why was he wasting time now on building the place? He had all the front he needed. All that remained was a sucker with enough money.

Yet that might take a long time and he was a fool to wait. He had a feeling his luck was running out, and it was the sort of hunch to which he had always paid attention in the past.

He went up the stairs to his room and looked around gloomily. It was empty as a barn . . . no place for a man to live. And nothing for him downstairs but coffee and a talk with John Brennan.

He glanced at the two books thrust down into his unstrapped pack—purposely he had left it open for the last few items. He had always wanted to read more, but there had never seemed to be time. Yet he knew that was not true, either—there was always time. One simply had to make time, and there was always a lot a man did that was trifling and altogether unimportant.

Thoughts of the town crowded his mind. Red Horse was booming, and he had done this; but now he was impatient, knowing he should be on his way, knowing he had stayed far too long. He had the uncomfortable feeling that things were bunching up on him.

There was one thing he could do, and he did it. He put on his hat and went down the street and personally thanked each of the men who had stood with him against Buell and his crowd.

Al Damon was loafing in front of Pearly Gates' old place, now reopened as a saloon by a big burly man

called Spike Maloon. The sight of the boy made Fallon
nervous, for he knew what Damon was thinking. Had he
not been the son of one of those first settlers of Red
Horse, Macon Fallon would not have been disturbed,
but he felt he owed those men a debt, and he knew the
trouble that was wrapped up in Al Damon.

Damon turned to look at him as he approached, and
there was a challenge in his eyes. Fallon merely glanced
at him, saying, "Hello, Al." Then he paused momen-
tarily. "Riding in the hills lately?"

Al Damon had been building himself up to say something, to say anything to challenge this man. He kept
telling himself he had to kill him. Bellows wanted him
killed, and it was up to him to do it. But the sudden remark, dropped so casually into the pool of his small security, sent ripples that rocked his boat of assurance.

His mouth opened to speak. Did Fallon know? But
how could he? Had he been followed? Al felt a sudden
chill of apprehension . . . suppose Fallon told his father?

But Fallon had turned his back and gone into the saloon.

Spike Maloon was behind the bar, a powerful man
with great, square-knuckled fists and bulging biceps. He
took a cigar from between his white, even teeth and
looked Fallon over coolly. This was a man who had faced
much trouble and had handled it.

At a table sat a slender, wiry man who got up and
strolled to the bar. His features were narrow and hawk-
like, his eyes set too close together. Fallon glanced at
him, noting the way the gambler held his right hand.
Wearing a sleeve-gun, Macon, he told himself. *Watch
this one.*

"I'm Fallon," he said. "You can run this place as long

as you run it honest. One sound like a crooked game, and I'll close you up."

Across the street Joshua Teel had stopped by Al Damon. "Did Fallon go in there?" he asked.

"Yeah."

Teel turned his head and looked up the street to where Devol was loading some gear into a wagon. "Devol—come along down here, will you?"

Inside the saloon, the gambler looked at Fallon. "You are calling me dishonest?"

"I am calling you nothing. I know nothing about you. I am simply telling you."

"We heard you ran this town," Maloon said. "We are telling you now . . . you don't run this place. We don't pay your percentage. You won't close us up."

A faint smile crossed Fallon's face. "We will discuss that when the time comes," he said quietly. "As for collecting my percentage, I'll do that." He glanced at the gambler. "I like a little game myself once in a while."

The gambler smiled. "By all means . . . whenever you're in the mood."

When Fallon emerged upon the street he saw Teel and Devol waiting outside, ready to come in. "Thanks," he said. "Glad to have you on hand."

"Trouble?"

"There will be." He paused. "That gambler in there—that's Card Graham. He's killed two men over poker games, and at least one over a woman. If you hear any reports of cheating, have him brought to me. Pass the word around, will you?"

He started to turn away, but stopped. "He carries a sleeve-gun. When a man knows how to use it, it is the fastest draw there is."

"Fallon?"

He turned back to Devol. "Yes?"

"The big fellow in there—he won't fight with a gun. He makes a point of never carrying one. He's a bruiser."

Fallon considered that. "Do you know him?"

"He was one of John Morrissey's roughnecks back in New York. He belonged to one of the fire companies who fought against Poole and that crowd."

Macon Fallon remembered the tremendous brawls in New York some years before, when the rival factions of Morrissey and Poole had met in the streets. Morrissey had, at one time, claimed the heavyweight championship of the world, and was a noted brawler who later founded the gambling in Saratoga and became an important man in New York politics.

Men were frequently killed in those brawls, to say nothing of the ears torn off, the eyes gouged, or the ugly scars left by teeth or stabbing thumbnails. If Spike Maloon was a graduate of that school, he was a tough man.

"Get out of here, you damned fool!" Fallon told himself as he walked away. "Get out while the getting's good."

But he did not go. He told himself several times a day he was a fool, but he still stayed on.

The truth was, he liked the place. The town was growing and, following his example, several of the new residents had begun to plant gardens, trim trees, and generally make the place more attractive.

There was little trouble in town. The residents were mostly a hard-working lot, and family men. The few drunks were usually passing through, and it was rarely necessary to do more than suggest they go to bed.

But it was too good to last.

Trouble began suddenly. A wagon, only a mile the other side of the bridge, was attacked and three people slain.

Everybody in Red Horse heard the shot, but when they arrived on the scene, the man, his wife, and young son were dead, the wagon looted, the horses driven off. It might have been Utes, but several of the riders rode shod horses.

"Stolen horses, probably," Blane suggested. "Ridden by Indians."

"Or by white men," Fallon said grimly. "This is a typical Bellows stunt."

And then came the night when Al Damon killed a man.

The wagons arrived just before sundown. They were mostly freighters, but several wagons of men with families headed for Oregon had joined the freighters for protection. One of these was a man of about forty, a tall, lean man, who came into town for a drink.

He stopped at Maloon's place, had one drink, and then another. During the time he was there he had nothing to say, but when he left the shadowed saloon and stepped out into the bright sunlight he ran into Al Damon.

He had come out of the saloon fast, like a man who had just remembered something, and when he bumped into Al Damon he staggered Al, knocking him back two steps.

Al swore and grabbed for his gun. Even as his hand grasped the butt, something inside him seemed to scream *No! No!*, but he had been thinking of it too long: the gun swung up and he looked across it into the startled eyes of the stranger.

"Please! I didn't mean—"

The gun in Al's hand seemed to cough, and the man turned around and fell against the side of the building. Then slowly, he sagged down to his knees.

Somewhere a woman screamed and people came running. The woman threw herself upon the fallen man, screaming and crying, as the stranger again turned half around and, looking at Al Damon with awful, staring eyes he said, "I'm sorry. I didn't mean . . ."

The man died that way, against the building, his wife clutching him, her body shuddering with wild sobs. He died with his eyes on Al Damon.

"Look," Al protested, "I didn't—" but nobody was paying any attention.

"He was packing a gun!" Al's tone had become pleading. "I saw his gun."

Joshua Teel turned from the dead man. "Buttoned into its holster. He was looking for somebody to fix it. Had a broke firing pin."

"How could I know that?" Al protested. "I—"

"You've been hunting it," Budge from the café interrupted. "For days now you've been swaggering around, playing tough, letting everybody see you were carrying a gun. Well, now you've killed a man . . . a man who did nobody any harm. You made a widow and three orphans."

"You murdered him," Hamilton said. "That there was murder."

Al Damon backed off. He was suddenly sick inside, and he knew he was about to throw up. He had to get off the street before that happened. Abruptly, he turned into an alleyway.

He had killed a man.

He half fell against the building and was sick. How could he know the man was carrying a useless gun? The man had shoved him . . . well, it seemed like that, anyway.

He wiped his mouth with the back of his hand and went around behind the buildings.

He wanted to go home, but the thought of his mother's eyes stopped that idea. Instead, he climbed over the corral bars and went into the stable, where he crawled back on the freshly cut hay and put his back against the wall.

The staring eyes of the dying man and those frightful sobs stayed with him. He cowered there, and finally he slept.

When he awoke it was dark. He listened for some sound, but heard nothing. He crawled out of the hay and carefully brushed himself off; and then he thought of his gun, and he reloaded the empty chamber.

Well, suppose he did kill that stranger? He asked for it, didn't he? He came barreling out of that door and almost knocked him down. Why, when it came to that, he had acted in self-defense. Looked like he was being jumped on—how was he to know?

He looked down at his gun. He had killed a man. He could file a notch on it now. The momentary twinge he had felt was stifled by a growing pride. It wasn't everybody could say that . . . that they'd killed a man.

When he got back on the street he hitched his gun a little farther forward. All right . . . so let them talk. If they got tough with him he'd . . .

The street was empty. Lights shone from a few windows. It was after suppertime and he was hungry. He went into the restaurant.

Two strangers were there, and both got up very pointedly and walked toward the door, leaving their food. Budge came from the kitchen with coffee just as they were leaving. "Hey, here's your coffee!" he called.

"Forget it," one man said. "We'd rather go hungry."

Al Damon felt the blood rising to his face. Should he call them on that? He started to turn, uncertain as to what he should do, when Budge spoke.

"Get out," he said coldly, "and don't come in here again. We don't serve your kind."

Al hesitated, appalled and angry. Budge stooped and took a double-barreled shotgun from under the counter. "Get going," he said. "If it was up to me, there'd be a hanging party tonight."

Al walked out onto the street. They couldn't talk that way to him! Just wait—he'd show them!

He needed a horse—above all things, he needed a horse. To hell with them! He would ride and join Bellows!

But where to go now? He still had no desire to go home, and he suspected the feeling evidenced by Budge would be present almost everywhere. And then he thought of the Yankee Saloon.

Fallon would probably be there. He might not be, but if he was, it was high time they met, for now they would meet on a new footing. Fallon must respect him now. Moreover, Brennan was a man who censured no man. Even in the short time since his arrival in Red Horse, his philosophy had become known. John Brennan turned no man from his bar.

Al had taken only a few steps when a voice stopped him. It was Lute Semple.

"You're pretty fast with that gun, Al. I saw that. You slicked it out mighty fast."

Al Damon shrugged, standing wide-legged on the walk. "He came for me," he said.

"What I hear," Semple said dryly. "When we heard about it, we figured it was Fallon you'd killed." He paused to let the idea sink in. "Could have been, you know. The same way. It would work on him better than on Bates."

"Who's Bates?"

"The man you killed." Lute Semple waited for a moment, and then added: "He was a well-liked man. He'd two brothers back in Illinois that set store by him."

"What's that to me?"

"You ain't used to it yet, kid. Why, those brothers, they'll come huntin' you. You'll have to keep a sharp eye out from now on."

Al shifted his feet uneasily. "What did you mean, it would work on Fallon easier than Bates?"

"It's an easy thing to let a man bump into you or, if there's nobody around, to let on the other man drew first. That Fallon . . . he doesn't have many friends.

"Bates was nobody. Fallon, now, that's a different story." Lute Semple paused. "Bellows, he's all for lettin' Tandy Herren come into town, and Tandy wants to come. Only I figured you should have your chance."

Semple struck a match to the stub of a cigar. "Far as that goes, we could give you a mite of help. Not that you'd need help, but insurance that don't cost nothin' is another thing."

"Where would you be?"

"That store across from the Yankee's got an upper story with nobody in it. A couple of us with Winchesters could come up the back stairs and we could lay there. When Fallon came out the door, you could bump him and draw, and when you did, we'd cut down on him from the window. Then we'd down the steps and high-tail it."

———

MACON FALLON WAS at breakfast at his usual table in the Yankee Saloon when Wiley Pollock came in. Pollock was a tall, strapping young man with a genial expression that masked an underlying seriousness.

"Are you Mr. Fallon?" Pollock asked. "They tell me you have some mining claims for sale."

Fallon allowed no hint of his elation to come into his expression. "Well, let's put it this way. I have some claims. I won't say they're for sale. On the other hand, I was never much of a man to dig, so if the price was right I might talk about it."

He refilled his coffee cup and then pushed another cup toward Pollock. "Are you a miner?"

"Not exactly," Pollock replied, "but I came west to mine, not farm." He looked sharply at Fallon. "Nobody seems to be mining . . . why?"

"My fault. A town isn't built by people who want to get rich overnight. I wanted some business going here first; but personally," he added, "I have been doing some development and exploration on my claims."

They talked for half an hour, and then together they went up the hill to the mine.

Wiley Pollock looked around thoughtfully. It was obvious that some work had been done. The tools stood about, and also the wheelbarrow Fallon had used. There was fresh rock thrown on the dump. Pollock went into the tunnel and knocked off a couple of chunks of rock and studied them.

Fallon stooped suddenly and picked up a piece of rock, glanced at it quickly, and thrust it into his pocket.

"May I see that?" Pollock extended his hand.

"It was nothing," Fallon said, with studied carelessness, "nothing at all."

Pollock walked out into the sun and looked around again. "How much are you asking?" he said.

Fallon shook his head. "I am sorry. I don't believe I will sell. I'll admit," he said, "I'm not a miner, and I have been ready to sell if the price was right, but I don't think I'll sell . . . not yet."

Pollock looked at him shrewdly. "Have anything to do with that rock you picked up back there?"

"No . . . no, of course not."

"I'll give you three thousand cash," Pollock said.

"Sorry."

Macon Fallon looked down the street. *Three thousand?* It was a good bit of money. *Take it, and run.* The thought went through his mind, but he dismissed the idea.

At the door of the Yankee Saloon, Fallon paused. "I might go higher," Pollock suggested.

"It would have to be much higher," Fallon responded. And then he pushed through the door and went in. At the bar, he said to Brennan, "John, let me have your hammer."

Pollock still stood on the boardwalk out front. He heard the back door close, then the sound of a hammer on rock, several blows, and then a grating sound. After a few minutes Fallon came back through the saloon, leaving the hammer on the bar as he went through. He crossed the street to Damon's store.

"Get out your gold scales, Damon. I want to weigh up a little."

Fallon took out the gold he had collected at the mountain spring. In most gold camps a teaspoonful was calculated as an ounce, and he had less than that, but it would be more than enough.

"Half-ounce," Damon said, "a mite over. My guess would be twelve dollars."

"All right."

Damon paid over the twelve dollars and Fallon slipped it into his pocket.

"Get that on your claim?" Damon asked.

Fallon chuckled. "One piece of rock . . . no bigger than your fist."

Damon's eyes tried to shield his interest. "Much of it around?"

Fallon shrugged. "Probably not . . . float, more than likely."

He crossed the street and went into the Yankee Saloon again, and within a few minutes he saw Pollock go into the store across the way. Smiling to himself, he went to the back and sat down. Brennan's eyes followed him.

Joshua Teel came in, and Budge followed. "Mr. Fallon, are you busy?" Budge said.

"What is it?"

"Maloon's place. Card Graham's making trouble. He rooked a couple of newcomers last night, then laughed at them when they called him on it."

"He didn't shoot?"

"They weren't heeled. But I think they'll be back."

Fallon looked down at his coffee. He had told them

what he would do. Of course, he had seen nothing, but it sounded to him like a deliberate challenge. But what about the men he rooked? Would they come back?

"You saw them," he said to Teel. "Will they come back?"

"They'll come. He trimmed them good, and didn't seem to care whether they knew it or not."

Macon Fallon got to his feet. "I'll talk to Graham." He stepped outside and looked down the street. He could see the wagons of the newcomers on the flat below the town.

Across the street, on the upper floor of the building, Lute Semple pointed at him. "See?" he said. "He's right where I want him. You call him, I shoot him. Everybody will think it was you. But you shoot twice, d'you hear? And miss that second shot so there'll be a place for mine if they try to figure it out."

"Yours might be in the back."

"That's why I say your second should miss. You can claim your first shot turned him. But maybe I can get a bullet into him in front . . . I'll try."

Down in the street Macon Fallon straightened his hat. "I'll talk to Graham," he said, "and Maloon."

"You'd best hurry, then," Teel replied grimly, "for here they come!"

Two men were walking up the street, both of them with guns strapped on. They were some distance off, but they walked in step and with determination, and they looked neither to right nor left.

Several men stepped out on the boardwalk as they passed, and a woman or two. The story had gotten around, and everyone knew what was happening. Fallon quickened his step, but he was too late. The two men did a perfect flanking movement at the door, and one of them reached up to push the door open.

The double-barreled shotgun blast ripped through the door and drove the man backward into the street. Graham had fired, and then reaching up, caught a second shotgun tossed to him by Maloon. Instantly he was at the door, firing again.

The second man, shocked by the coughing bellow of the shotgun and by his friend's sudden death, hesitated that fraction of a second that made him too late. The blast the second shotgun threw at him tore him in two.

Macon Fallon spoke quietly. "Empty now, isn't it?"

Card Graham seemed to wince, then he turned his head slowly, as a rattler may turn at some uncertain danger.

"Don't drop it," Fallon said. "If you do I might think you're going for a gun." Without turning his head, he said, "Teel, take the rear door. If he makes a wrong move, kill him."

He walked up slowly and said, "We'll go inside, Card. Poker is your game, isn't it?"

Graham stared at him. "You want to *play?*"

"Yes . . . if we can call it play. Yes, I want to play."

Wiley Pollock was there. Fallon saw him looking on, coolly interested.

"Pollock," he said, "let me have your best offer, your final offer for the claim."

"Ten thousand dollars," Pollock replied promptly. "In cash, now."

"Done," Fallon replied.

"I don't get it," Graham was saying. "Why play now?"

Fallon felt cold and still inside. He felt the way he

sometimes had before a gun battle, but he felt something more. He felt hatred.

He knew neither man who had died, but he had seen them both come into town. They were good men, solid men . . . and both had families.

"You owe those men something," he said quietly, "and they have families. I am going to win it for them."

Card Graham laughed without humor. "Don't be a fool, Fallon. You owe them nothing. Stay out of this."

He said it as a matter of course. What he wanted very much was what he was going to get—Macon Fallon in a card game. He did not know Fallon, but he did not like him.

Fallon followed Graham into the saloon and took a seat at a table with his back to the wall. Card Graham sat down opposite him and took a deck of cards from a box on the table. Graham drew high card, and the deal.

He shuffled the cards, Fallon cut, and Graham dealt. "We do not stop," Fallon said, "until one of us is broke, and if you go broke, you leave town."

Graham did not reply. Cards were his game, cards were what he knew. He had started playing in a Texas cow camp shortly after coming down from Ohio; he had continued to play in cow camps for a year, then opened a game in a cow town. He had picked up a little here, a little there. He had never played the riverboats, never the big places in St. Louis or Chicago or New York, but he was very sure of himself.

They played, and Graham won. He won steadily for an hour, and he was playing a fair game. He knew it, and Macon Fallon knew it.

Then the cards took a change, and they took the change while Graham was dealing. Fallon found himself with good cards, decided it was not a set-up situation and played it to win. Graham had a fair hand, thought Fallon was bluffing, and lost almost a third of what he had won up to that moment.

Irritated, Graham played the next hand badly and won, but much less than he should have with the cards he held.

An hour later Fallon was winning steadily, and Card Graham suggested drinks. Spike Maloon came around the bar with the drinks on a tray and Macon Fallon glanced up, smiling faintly. He lifted a hand. "Put the tray down on the next table," he said quietly. "We can take our drinks from there."

There was silence in the room. Card Graham's face paled slightly. "What's that mean?" His eyes were hot and eager.

A killer, Fallon thought. *The man's become a killer. He's begging for a chance to draw his gun.*

"I'm superstitious," Fallon said, "about trays. I don't like trays near the table while I'm playing." He smiled into Graham's eyes. "I know this is an honest game, but sometimes a tray can have a cold deck under it."

Graham wanted to say something, but he hesitated, and Macon Fallon knew why he hesitated. There was a cold deck under that tray, and if he said anything Fallon would suggest the tray be turned over.

"Forget it!" Graham said, shrugging. "Let's play cards."

Fallon was looking away from the table when he heard the faint whisper of a bottom deal. The sliding of that bottom card off the end of the pack had a faintly different sound, but he did not react. When he picked up his cards he was holding three nines. He discarded two cards and was given two more, and one of them was the other nine.

He folded his cards together and raised another two dollars. Graham seemed to be studying his cards, which gave Fallon time to think.

Three nines was logical. It was the sort of hand a fairly careful card mechanic might give, enough to make him raise, yet not too big. The fourth nine was not logical.

Fallon studied Card Graham in his mind and decided the fourth nine was an accident. The deck, he was sure, was not marked. The nines would be unlikely marking in any event, for usually that was reserved for face cards, aces, and tens—although complete marking had often been done. It was probable that Graham figured the chance of his getting that extra nine was impossibly high . . . and it was unlikely. Yet unlikely things were always happening in poker games.

Graham raised ten dollars, and Fallon upped it one hundred. Graham's face was unreadable, but Fallon had an idea Graham was pleased, for it must seem that Fallon had taken the bait. Macon Fallon smiled inwardly—and grimly, for perhaps he had. He was betting that the fourth nine was an accident.

Graham saw his raise and boosted it five hundred.

At the showdown, Graham showed a full house, queens and jacks, and Fallon spread out his four nines.

Card Graham stared unbelievingly at the cards as Fallon raked in the money. His tongue touched his lips, for he knew how great the odds were against Fallon's picking up that fourth nine on the draw. But Fallon had done it, and there was no way it could have been rigged, because Fallon could not have known what cards Graham would give him.

Fallon watched Graham with seemingly casual interest. The fun was over. Card Graham had been hurt where he liked it least—in his skill as a card mechanic. From now on, it would be every man for himself.

Idly, Fallon gathered the cards, shuffled, pushed them over for Graham's cut, then dealt. Fallon was a good poker player, but few card sharps were, for they were too busy building up a chance to cheat, or watching for that chance . . . and they are depending on cheating to win, not on good poker playing. Yet a good card mechanic need cheat only once in a game, if he chooses the right time.

Fallon bluffed on a small pair, but Graham was no longer sure, and would not go along.

Fallon was keenly aware of Graham's problems. It takes time to get the cards in place for a crooked deal, and it is easier when the game is stud and some of the cards can be seen each time a hand is played, exposed on the table and easy for the pick-up. At stud it is comparatively easy to follow the cards one wants, separate and stock them for a bottom deal. In draw poker the selection is limited by the number of cards that can be seen, for unless a cold deck can be introduced into the game, the necessary cards must be located and stocked.

Also, the fewer involved in the game the fewer the cards that can be seen. Fallon wondered which ones Graham would select. His own elaborate appearance of ease was deliberately calculated to infuriate the gambler.

The game seesawed back and forth. For a while others joined in, but the contest was so obviously between the two men that they were glad to get out. Everybody in

Red Horse knew the game was on, and everybody knew it could only end in trouble.

Spike Maloon sat or walked behind the bar and watched the progress of the game with cynical eyes. They were eyes that had looked upon much that was evil, little that was good, and upon many men who were hard, brutal men in their hours of trial. More and more he found his eyes shifting to Macon Fallon.

His own future rode with Graham's winning, but as the hours passed he saw that Graham was playing a losing game. The cards were erratic, no long winning streaks coming to either man, with Graham unable to control them as he wished. And even when he could, Fallon seemed to pull away from every trap by instinct as much as by card sense.

There was nothing Maloon could do. He had brought the cold deck to the table, but Fallon had been ready for them, so he could only sit it out. Men came and went; gradually as the night wore on they tired out and the crowd dwindled. Joshua Teel remained. Devol left, but Riordan came. And when the Yankee Saloon closed, John Brennan came down to Maloon's place.

Card Graham was sweating. He could make nothing work for him tonight, but half an hour ago he had stolen an ace, and now he had another. Three times he had set Fallon up for a trimming, and each time he had failed. He had managed to give him a full house, only to have Fallon discard and ask for three cards. He caught himself just as he was about to look up, like any greenhorn.

Fallon had a memory for cards. It was a priceless asset to a gambler, and Fallon suddenly realized that it had been some time since he had seen the ace of diamonds. He picked up the deck . . . thin . . . it was a thin deck.

One or two cards were gone. A gambler learns to judge such things, but even though he might be wrong, he was not prepared to risk it.

He put the cards down. "This deck is bad luck," he declared. "Neither of us has done any good with it. Let's have a new deck."

Graham felt a sudden surge of viciousness, and a wild impulse to leap up and slap Fallon across the mouth. Two aces out, and a switch in decks!

On the back bar there was a pack of cards that had not been there when Maloon brought the tray to the table. They had appeared on the back bar right afterward. Undoubtedly this was the stacked deck they had tried to slip into the game.

As Maloon started to reach under the back bar for a deck of cards, Fallon indicated the deck on the back bar. "We'll use that one," he said.

Maloon hesitated the briefest instant, then brought the deck to the table. Graham started to interrupt, then stopped. It could be a trap. It could be a means of exposing him, for after all, this was his place. He was the gambler in this saloon.

As he took the deck Fallon managed a glance at the bottom card . . . a trey . . . an unlikely card for part of a bottom stock. The chances were that the arranged cards were at the top. As Graham had planned to cheat him, the first card was intended to go to the sucker, the second to the winner, and so forth.

Talking easily, Fallon took the deck, undercut about three-fourths of the deck, injogged the first card, and shuffled off to the break, then threw the remainder on top. He worked with the practiced skill of years, a skill that had worked on the riverboats and in the crowded gambling salons of New York, Saratoga, New Orleans, St. Louis and Cleveland.

He pushed the deck toward Graham for the cut, talking as he did so. Graham cut the deck and Fallon picked it up, commented on the gun a spectator was wearing, and at the same time did a one-hand shift of the cut, shielding the move with his right hand as they came together.

Shifting the cut was a standard practice of the skilled card sharp, for a stacked deck is relatively useless without returning the cut cards to their original position. Fallon knew half a dozen methods, but preferred the one-hand shift.

The packet of cards that he wanted on top had to go on the bottom when picked up, so as he brought the two packets together in his left hand he held a slight break open between them with his second finger. It required much practice to tilt the bottom half of the deck and slide the upper packet beneath it, but it could be done instantaneously, returning the cards to their original arrangement before the cut was made.

Light was just breaking in the street outside when Fallon dealt the hand. Card Graham stared at his cards, then threw them aside in disgust, recognizing them as the hand he had set up in the cold deck for Fallon. Fallon simply grinned, raking in the few chips.

Half an hour later he saw his chance. Graham had won two small pots by straight poker, and was beginning to feel his luck had changed. He also won a third hand, with a full house, aces and queens.

As Fallon swept the cards together, he noted the position of the aces, including one from his own hand, and the queens. He did a fast cull shuffle, picking up the other two queens in the process, and after the cut did another one-hand shift of the cut. When he dealt the cards, he gave Graham three queens.

As for himself, he held his cards, staring at them, glancing at the pot, at Graham, finally seeing Graham's bet and raising. On the draw he gave Graham the fourth queen and another card, taking two cards himself. On the showdown, with two thousand dollars in the pot, he showed four aces to Graham's four queens.

Graham stared at the cards, his face slowly turning pale and ugly. When he looked up at Fallon his eyes were vicious. "Why, you—!"

Macon Fallon had never felt more calm, more ready. "You killed two men, Graham, after cheating them of their money. You tried to cheat me, but you're small-time, Graham. You aren't really good with cards, and you never will be. On the River they would laugh at you.

"Now I am going to give you a chance. *I am going to give you ten minutes to get out of town!*"

Card Graham was trembling inside, trembling with hatred and bitterness, and yet with eagerness. He was going to kill Fallon. He was going to shoot him in the guts and let him die slow.

He reached for his hat with his left hand and picked it up. He brought it across in front of him and reached for the edge with his right hand, as though to put his hat on with both hands. His right hand disappeared behind the hat, and Macon Fallon shot him.

Fallon's gun blasted, tearing a hole in the crown of Graham's hat and driving the middle button on his belt back into his belly.

The hat fell, revealing Graham's smashed hand and

bloody fingers and the half-drawn derringer fastened by a metal clip to his left wrist, under the coat sleeve.

Graham backed up, fell to the edge of a chair and it turned over, spilling him to the floor. He bumped the table as he fell, and a black ace fell with him.

Macon Fallon watched the group of men carefully. His eyes went from one to another, but no one spoke until Riordan said, "He had his gun in his hand when you shot him."

Fallon stood up and gathered the money from the table. He then put all he had won on the table and split it into three equal piles. One of these he pocketed.

"Josh," he said, "each one of those widows gets one of these, and if they will stay in Red Horse we will find homes for them."

"They didn't lose anywhere near that much," Teel said.

"They lost their husbands in my town," Fallon replied shortly. "Take it to them."

Fallon walked out into the street and squinted his eyes against the morning sun. He was suddenly tired, very tired. But he had his stake. With the price of the claim he had sold, with the money won in the game with Graham, he had at least twelve thousand dollars.

He could go now. He was through here.

CHAPTER 6

MACON FALLON STOOD at the window of his rooms above the Yankee Saloon and looked down the street of the town he had created from the ashes of fraud. His eyes were cynical, his mouth twisted wryly. Tomorrow he would ride out. It would be hours before they realized he was not coming back.

Red Horse had served him well, but he needed it no longer, and the bright lights of San Francisco and the Palace Hotel were calling. Disturbingly, he found his eyes hesitating over the fields, now green with crops.

The water supply was not to be depended on, so what they must do was drill a well or two down on the flat. There was a good chance of hitting water there, close under the mountain's edge.

The town needed a shoemaker, too. Maybe the harnessmaker could take it on. It also needed a tailor, and an effort should be made to get one out here.

He swore suddenly, angry with himself for his foolish thoughts. Once Pollock found out there was no gold on his claim, the lid would blow off and the people would be gone, even faster than they had left before. His only chance would be to get out first, before they discovered the town was based on a lie.

He glanced down at his gear. He would need another canteen, a little more food. He put on his hat and went down the stairs, nodding to Brennan as he passed. Brennan put his cigar down on the edge of the bar and watched Fallon down the street. Brennan's eyes showed worry.

Fallon crossed the street and went into the Damon store. He was well inside the door before he saw that the store was empty except for Ginia Blane, who was behind the counter.

He started to go out, but her voice stopped him. "Mr. Fallon, is there something I can do for you?"

Turning back, he walked to the counter. "Yes." He spoke shortly, crisply, wanting no talk. "You can sell me a canteen. I notice you have several in stock."

"Of course." She looked into his eyes. "Are you going somewhere?"

Damn the girl! He flashed her an angry look before he could put a guard on his feelings, then he replied, "Oh, I scout around the country a good deal, and I want to look over the desert west of here."

She got the canteen for him and filled his other requests. He commented on her working in the store.

"Mr. Damon is in the fields today, and Al won't help him, so he hired me." She looked into his eyes again. "You must be careful. Al Damon does not like you."

He was surprised at her warning. "I should think it would please you if something happened to rid the town of me."

"Indeed, it would not. We need you."

"The town needs no one." He gathered his purchases. He hesitated an instant, suddenly reluctant to leave. Glancing at her, he surprised her blue eyes wide with some unexpected emotion, and it startled and upset him. He glanced hurriedly away. "There is no such thing as an indispensable man."

"You are wrong. There are often indispensable men." She stepped closer to the counter. "Mr. Fallon, I have much to learn, and some of it Mr. Teel has been explaining to me. I know what you did with that money you won. I know why you played that game, risking all you had."

"I played it to win," he said. "Graham was not the sort of man a town needs."

She frowned at him. "I can't begin to understand you, Mr. Fallon. You are a gambler, and yet in this town you have tolerated no gamblers. You have deliberately chosen men who have trades, substantial men."

"Gamblers are birds of passage. I am a bird of passage."

"And so you would leave us?"

"I've said nothing about leaving," he replied impatiently, "but what difference would it make if I did? The first time they had a chance to be rid of me, they tried it. They will try again."

"Feelings change. I believe the attitude has changed here."

She came from behind the counter and he walked a step or two toward the door, but she came up to him. "I think you are a fraud, Mr. Fallon. I think you are a tremendous fraud!"

His smile was sardonic. "I thought you knew that . . . you accused me of switching the town's name for some . . . some reason or other."

"I do not mean that. I think you are a fraud, Mr. Fallon, because I believe you are a good man and a good citizen masquerading as a gambler, a cheat, and a drifter."

"You talk like a fool!" he said sharply. "You're a romantic child!"

He stepped outside quickly before she could say more, and walked swiftly up the street. He swore bitterly. Damn the girl.

Suddenly he paused. One more thing he would do. He would close out Maloon.

Turning on his heel, he went down the street and entered the saloon. There were half a dozen men drinking at the bar. The card tables were empty.

He wasted no time. "Maloon, you tossed that shotgun to Graham. I heard of that. You tolerated his presence here. We do not want your kind. Brennan will buy you out for what you have invested . . . then get out."

Spike Maloon took the cigar from his mouth and squinted through the smoke.

"And if I do not?"

"We will run you out."

"*We?*" Spike Maloon picked up his cigar and glanced at it. "You would need help, of course. I never use a gun, so you'd have no excuse to use one on me."

"You have been told. Now sell out, and get out."

"Too bad," Maloon said, running his eyes over Fallon. "I'd not have believed you were yellow. You stand up pretty well, good shoulders, good hands. I would have guessed you could take care of yourself. But you always have that gun to hide behind . . . and now you hide behind this '*we*' you speak of.

"But it is just as well. You'd have no more chance with me with your hands than I would with you with a gun."

Fallon knew he was being baited, deliberately baited by a man who was positive of what he could do. There were others standing about, but he knew they expected nothing of him. No doubt there was not a man present who would not think him wise to leave things as they were.

Yet there was a lurking devil of Irish madness in him, and he looked at Spike Maloon with real pleasure. "It is a foolish thing you do," he said cheerfully, "to challenge me in this way. You have a reputation as a fearful man with your fists, Spike Maloon, and when it comes to that, you have nothing else. Lose that, and you will have nothing at all. It is not a thing to be lightly risked."

Spike Maloon's surprise did not show on his face, but surprised he was, and profoundly. He had it in mind to dare Fallon into a fight and then whip him within an inch of his life—destroy him, in fact. Yet Fallon's way of rising to the bait made him wary . . . could the man fight, then?

"I'll lose nothing. The man never lived who could handmuck a Maloon, but if you've a mind to fight, then stack your duds and grease your skids, for I shall tear down your meat-house!"

Suddenly, Macon Fallon felt good. He felt fine. This was a fitting thing, this last bit he could do for Red Horse, and for himself as well. For weeks now he had been a discontented man, with much wearing on his mind, and not always certain of the way to go. But in a fight, a slam-bang, knock-down and drag-out fist fight there were no complications. It was root-hog or die, and suddenly and with pleasure, he took off his gun belt.

In an instant the yell went up the street, "*Fight! Fight! It's Fallon and Maloon! . . . Fight!*"

And they came running—from all the corners of town they came running.

At the Yankee Saloon, John Brennan heard the cry

and turned around so sharply that the ash fell from his cigar. "The man's daft!" he exclaimed. "He's bloody daft!"

Devol started to his feet to rush to the fight, but Teel's voice brought him up short. "Think, man!" he yelled. "Remember what we were told!"

Brennan grabbed up a bucket and caught up some water in it, and then filled a bottle with it, fresh and cold. With a towel over his arm, he started down the street, not forgetting the lock on the door he closed behind him.

Spike Maloon was stripped to the waist in the street and Macon Fallon was carefully folding his coat over the hitch rail when Brennan arrived.

"He has forty pounds on you," Brennan said, "as well as height and reach. Is there a way out, then?"

"Through him," Fallon replied, grinning. "The way out is through him. The only way out is to tear him apart or beat him down, for he stands across my way."

"Have at it, then, but he has a jaw like granite, I've heard. You'd best not waste your hands on it."

It looked as if the whole town was there, and not the last was Ginia Blane, for she left the store almost running, slamming the door locked behind her. Something winked at the corner of her eye as she ran, some sudden flash of sunlight, but she gave it no thought.

Lute Semple was on the upper floor with a mirror, playing the flash against the far-off hills. A moment later there came an answering flash, and he put the mirror down and picked up his rifle, checking the load.

He glanced at the sun . . . how long would it take them? "Make it last, Fallon," he whispered to himself. "Make it last!"

Macon Fallon stripped to the waist and accepted from Brennan a pair of driving gloves, into which he slipped his hands.

Maloon looked at them and laughed. "You're a fool, man," he said. "They'll do you no good."

"What is it?" Budge demanded. "To a finish?"

"How else?" Fallon said, and moved up to the scratch.

Maloon was a towering big man, his skin as white as a woman's, but he was muscled like a Hercules. His hands were huge, and the knuckles bore the scars of many battles. He put up his hands and Macon Fallon moved into him, a dancing devil in his eyes, in his heart a sudden wild urge to slaughter, to destroy.

He feinted with his left, then followed through with it and the knuckles of his fist smashed against Maloon's teeth and jolted the bigger man to his heels.

"So it's a boxer you are? It's the kind I like," Maloon said. "I eat 'em alive!"

Fallon feinted again, swung hard with a right, and the fist that struck him came out of nowhere. It struck the side of his face like a bludgeon, and his feet flipped up and he hit the dust. Dazed, he looked up to see Maloon rushing in.

The big man dove at him and Fallon swung up a leg. His foot caught Maloon in the stomach, and he went on over Fallon to land in a heap. Fallon scrambled to his feet, still dazed, and saw Maloon turn head over heels like an acrobat and come to his feet.

"You've the makings of a fighter, lad," Maloon said. "Too bad I shall have to destroy you!"

He stepped in quickly, hitting hard with both hands. Fallon partially blocked the first punch but caught the second on the jaw, and his head rang. A light seemed to burst and shower him with its fragments. He ducked inside another punch, drove his head against Maloon's chest, then ripped up with his skull in the vicious "Liverpool kiss" known to rough-and-tumble fighters everywhere.

Maloon's head was smashed back by the impact of the skull under the chin, and Fallon sprang in, swinging incredibly fast with both fists. The blows landed, rocking Maloon's big head with their power and staggering him. In close then, Fallon followed through with an elbow smash to the face and stepped back.

As he did so, a stone rolled under his foot and a smashing fist caught him in the mouth. He tasted blood, and a wild, fierce urge to kill came up within him. He tried to butt again, was smashed back by a hamlike fist, drove in swinging, and had both blows blocked.

He tried another, and his right missed and went by, but he brought it around the big man's head, grabbed his own right wrist with his left hand and had a headlock on Maloon. Instantly he threw his feet in the air and sat down hard, trying to break Maloon's neck, but the big man was smart and went with him, and they fell together.

On the ground Maloon was a demon. Lightning fast, he swung around and stabbed a stiff thumb for Fallon's eye. Narrowly missing, the hard nail, deliberately scraped and filed until it had grown to unusual thickness and pointed as a weapon, ripped a gash in the side of Fallon's face from the corner of his eye almost back to his ear.

Wild with fear for his eyes, Fallon scrambled to get up, but Maloon got astride him and drew his big fist back for a killing blow. Fallon threw up his feet and caught

Maloon across the face with his crossed legs, snapping him back.

Torn loose from each other, both men scrambled to their feet, and Fallon ripped into Maloon, swinging with both fists, but Maloon stood his ground, punching hard and fast. The fists of both men were like clubs.

Toe to toe for almost a minute, they slugged wildly, then broke apart as if on command, and circled. Fallon's cut was bleeding badly; there was a huge welt under the other eye and a cut on his jaw. Maloon had an eye almost closed and a split lip.

They were fighting with animal ferocity, Maloon like a cornered grizzly, Fallon like a mountain lion. Fallon was relentless, always moving, always crowding; Maloon circled warily, quick to counter. Both were shrewd fighters, terrible fighters; both were victors in many a riverside or waterfront brawl.

They broke away from each other and each stepped to the side of the circle. Brennan doused Fallon with water, touched the bloody cut with the towel, dabbing away the blood. "Box him, man!" he whispered hoarsely. "That's a brute you have there!"

They came together, and Fallon feinted, then stabbed a left to the mouth. He slipped under a left and smashed a right to the ribs. He sidestepped as the big man threw a right, and countered swiftly, jolting Maloon. He started to sidestep again, caught a right, and was knocked down.

He dove away from a kick, came up to his knees, and as Maloon rushed him, swinging another kick, Fallon threw his weight against Maloon's anchored leg, knocking him down.

Maloon was up first, but Fallon swung his weight on his hands and kicked out behind him with both feet, kicking waist high in a move used by the French *la savate* fighters.

Both feet caught Maloon coming in and knocked him, sprawling and surprised, into a heap.

Fallon came up fast and swung a kick for Maloon's chin that missed as the big head ducked, but catching it with a glancing blow that sent Maloon sprawling into the dust again.

But Maloon was up and charging. His big head caught Fallon in the belly, smashing him back, every bit of wind knocked from him. Maloon's charge carried him on over Fallon, and he scrambled to his feet and turned to find Fallon staggering weakly to his feet.

Maloon rushed in, smashing a tremendous blow to Fallon's head that started him down. The second blow caught him falling and lost some of its force, but it laid Fallon's cheek open to the bone. He went down hard on his back and Maloon rushed in for the kill.

Unable to get up, Fallon rolled to left and right, trying desperately to avoid the kicks that might, any one of them, kill him or break his skull.

Staggering from the force of a kick, Maloon was carried on by him, and Fallon managed to get up. His lungs gasped for breath, every inhalation like a knife thrust into his chest. His head rang from the blows he had taken; he was punch-drunk with the fight. He had forgotten where he was or what was the issue at stake; he only knew that he must kill or be killed.

He waited, hands hanging, and Spike Maloon came to him. The big man had been shocked by the skill of Fallon, and by the force of the blows he had taken, but now he was sure. He had his man.

He was not only a big man, he was tremendously strong.

Now he struck a light blow to the face, testing Fallon's responses. He drew no return, but he was wary. He feinted a left, and then as Fallon struck out, he brushed the blow aside and knocked him down with his right. But Fallon, surprisingly, got up.

Spike Maloon was suddenly worried. He had struck with his hardest punches, and he had knocked Fallon down . . . time and again. But he always got up.

Now he must put him down and keep him down. This time he must put him on the ground, then jump on him and kick the life out of him, and quickly.

The watchers, hoarse from shouting, were silent now, shocked by the ferocity of the battle they watched. It was like two primeval men fighting far away in the past . . . like two utterly savage cavemen.

Maloon moved in. He had fought hard, but he had his second wind, and Fallon was finished. He struck out with a left . . . it landed. He struck again . . . it landed. He struck again . . . and suddenly his left arm was seized and he was thrown over Fallon's back with a flying mare. He hit the ground with a thud and Fallon fell upon him, a knee driving into his solar plexus as Fallon came down, then that same knee smashing up to hit his chin.

A terrible light burst in Maloon's skull. He fought himself free, and got up. His jaw was broken, smashed at the hinges and hanging free.

His hands . . . he had to get Fallon in his hands. Curling a bulky arm around his jaw, he charged to get close, swinging with his right fist.

Fallon brought up hard against the hitch rail and Maloon's big hand grasped his windpipe. Fallon tried to get at Maloon's eyes but the big man ducked his head low.

Lifting a boot, Fallon smashed down with the side of the boot against Maloon's shinbone, the heel driving down hard on Maloon's foot. But the bigger man clung grimly to his grip on the throat.

Fallon smashed up hard against Maloon's elbow, the elbow of the arm that was gripping his throat, and at the same time he reached over with his right hand and dug his fingers into the palm of the gripping hand. Retaining his hold, he ripped the hand free from his throat and, turning quickly, gripping the hand and pushing down on the elbow, he sent Maloon stumbling, bent over and head down. He fell, and lay still, face down in the dust.

Macon Fallon staggered toward him, then his knees folded and he fell. He tried to get up, and he fell again, and the last sound he heard was a rifle shot.

A rifle shot . . . and then another.

He fought his way out of a fog of unconsciousness and strained to get up. A gentle hand touched his shoulder and a voice whispered, "Lie still."

He relaxed slowly, trying to figure out where he was. It was dark, with strange faint streaks of light off to one side.

The voice . . . that had been Ginia. She was here with him.

Then he remembered the fight . . . but what happened after that? There had been a shot—after that he remembered nothing.

"Ginia?"

"Ssh!"

He whispered. "Where are we? What happened?"

"We were attacked . . . a lot of men on horseback. All of a sudden, just as your fight ended, they just came down out of nowhere, and there was a lot of shooting."

She stopped, listening. Then she added, "We're under the hotel."

There was, he recalled, a sort of hollow under the back of the hotel because it was built at a spot where the ground fell away behind it. The back of the hotel was actually resting on an eight-foot stone foundation.

Those strange streaks of light, he realized suddenly, could only be sunlight coming through the cracks in the boardwalk. It was alongside the boardwalk that he had fallen. As she could not have carried him, she must have come in through the back somehow and dragged him under the walk, and then down here.

"They were shooting and running their horses," she explained when he asked about it. "I was afraid you'd be killed." She paused a moment. "They are looking for you. Al Damon is with them."

"I thought as much." He lay quiet, trying to judge his own condition. His face felt stiff and sore, and he could move his jaw only with difficulty. One eye, he discovered, was swollen almost shut. He tried to work his fingers, but they, too, were stiff and sore.

"How long has it been?"

"An hour . . . maybe a little more."

"I've got to get a gun."

He was lying on his back and he turned over slowly and pushed himself to a sitting position. He felt sore all over. He could hear men moving about on the floor above, and they must be Bellows men, or there would be no reason to remain quiet.

He leaned close to Ginia. "Do you know what's happening now?"

"When they rode in," she said, "I know that somebody shot at them, because as they came around the corner we heard the shot and a man fell.

"Everybody scattered for shelter. They killed Mr. Hamilton, I think. You and Mr. Maloon were left lying there . . . I think they believed you had been killed. So I came around behind, got in here, and pulled you back under the walk. Then I spilled water from the trough over the ground where you had been dragged.

"They are looking for you now. I can hear what they say sometimes."

He sank back on the cool earth and looked up into the darkness that was the underside of the floor above. He could hear sporadic shooting, which meant the surprise had not been complete. Joshua Teel and some of those in his small band of defenders had been on the alert.

He must have a gun, that first of all. And then in some way he must get the defenders together and drive Bellows and his outfit from the town. At the same time, he must not risk Ginia's safety. But first of all, they must leave this place.

He sat up again, grasping her arm. There was an old door, he remembered, that opened at the back. It opened into a gully grown high with wiry brush and weeds, but there were paths through those weeds.

He got up and moved carefully in the darkness. He found the door, but there he hesitated. Did the hinges creak? No matter, he'd have to try it. He opened the door the merest crack and a bright glare of sunlight entered. It was a dozen feet to the brush. He tried to recall how many rear windows there were . . . surely they would be watched.

They stepped outside—then three running strides and they were in the brush, unseen, he hoped.

Beyond the gully the mountainside rose up. He must follow the gully, which grew more shallow farther on, and get into the Yankee Saloon if possible.

Somewhere a gun barked . . . two guns responded.

Crouched in the gully, they listened. The sun was blistering hot, the rocks too hot to touch. Lifting his head slowly, he peered out. Between two buildings he could see a section of the street. A dead horse lay there, and a man sprawled near the horse, a man with a bald head . . . a stranger.

Fallon looked up at the windows. At one of them he saw a gun barrel . . . was it friendly, or otherwise? He could not risk finding out.

His head ached with a dull, heavy throb, aggravated by the heat. He looked down at his hands, swollen out of shape, dark with bruises. He would have trouble with a pistol now, although he could manage it. A rifle . . . he wanted his Winchester.

He heard more shots, tried to locate their origin. Suddenly, he heard a faint creak of leather, and his breath caught. Then, carefully, he eased back to the deeper brush where Ginia waited.

Had he made any sound? He did not think so.

Under the baking sun he could smell the dust and the drying brush. He waited, motionless. Then he heard the footstep again, and suddenly the man came into view, not more than ten feet away.

He was a big bearded man, inclined to fatness around the midsection, and he carried a rifle and wore a belt gun. His eyes were small and mean—cruel eyes. It was obvious that he was hunting them . . . he had seen or heard something.

He slowly surveyed the brush. Fallon put his left hand back to touch Ginia, a warning. She was gone!

His hand closed on a jagged chunk of rock, and he started to lift it. As he did so, Ginia suddenly stood up, a dozen feet away, directly in front of the man with the rifle.

"Were you looking for me?" she said.

The man's rifle had started to come up, but at her words he lowered it. He moved toward her, and Fallon took three short, running steps and hit him in a long dive. Ginia had given Fallon his chance, and he had taken it.

His shoulder smashed into the man, hitting him just below the waist and lifting him almost bodily from the ground. The man fell sprawling, losing his grip on his rifle. Ginia caught it up and swung it by the barrel, a neat, precise swing that was like chopping cotton with a hoe. The solid *tunk* of the rifle butt against the man's skull was a welcome sound.

Swiftly, Fallon stripped the gun belt and holster from the man's waist, then took the rifle from Ginia.

Flattened against the side of the building, he glanced at her. "I thought you disapproved of violence?" he said softly.

Her chin lifted. "There are times," she said.

"Good girl," he whispered. "You think fast."

He checked the rifle. It was a .44 Henry, and the belt ammunition was .44 calibre.

Keeping close to the buildings, they ran toward the upper end of town. Fallon had a hunch that the defense would center there; he knew the best place to defend, the place from which the town could most easily be covered lay at the mining claim he had sold to Pollock. Next to that, the best place was the Yankee Saloon.

Brennan would at all costs head for there, and it was likely others would also, although the need to protect their families must of necessity scatter them.

Suddenly a shot nipped the wall near him, then another. Ducking between the buildings, Fallon saw a man in a dirty red shirt wheel to face him. As the man turned, a shot from somewhere laid a gash along the side of his neck. Fallon fired his Henry from the hip, and the bullet knocked the man sprawling back into the street, where another bullet finished the job.

"That came from the blacksmith shop," he said quietly.

They waited there between the buildings, and Fallon cursed himself for a fool. He should never have bothered with Spike Maloon, or allowed himself to be baited into a fight to the finish with him. He could have been miles from town, instead of stuck here in a defenseless position with a girl to take care of. Unless, he reflected, remembering the events of the last hour, it was she who took care of him.

The shooting ceased, and there was quiet.

Fallon glanced at the shadow of the building beside which he stood . . . the afternoon was well advanced, and with night the smaller numbers of the defenders, with their wives, children, and property to defend, would have small chance. Whatever was to be done must be done now. Undoubtedly Bellows was delaying for just that reason.

Ginia suddenly stood up. "Mr. Fallon, we need to know where our friends are, don't we?"

"That's it," he agreed. Then he indicated the shadow

of the building. "It grows late. If they can hold us off until dark, we'll not have much of a chance. If I could get to Teel and the others—Shelley, Riordan, Devol, and Yearly—I think we could run them out."

"Where do you think they are?"

He thought for a moment. "I'm guessing that your pa made it back to the blacksmith shop . . . Jim will be with your ma and the others, right behind the shop. They will be able to help each other that way.

"Our headquarters was the Yankee, and Brennan would try to get back there, but he may not have made it. The others—unless they went to their families—would be with Brennan. So I've got to get to the Yankee Saloon. More than that, wherever they are, they've got to know what I'm planning. If they aren't in the Yankee, they'll be at my old claim at the end of the street . . . we worked out an agreement."

She faced him. "I will find out for you."

"Don't be a fool."

"I am not." She looked at him coolly. "Mr. Fallon, I have been told that I am pretty. I am also young. You warned Pa and the others that when Bellows came he would be after women . . . in that case I don't believe he would shoot me."

He leaned back against the building and looked at her with respect. "You know," he said, "you're quite a girl."

"Thank you. . . . I will go out on the street, and I will walk up the street to the Yankee Saloon, seeing everything I can. When I get there I will have them fire a quick shot for every man there."

"There's a catch to this. Suppose they put a gun on you and tell you to come to them—or else?"

"I shall have to keep walking. I must chance it."

He nodded. "I'll say this for you. You've got sand. You've got nerve."

She held out her hand and looked him in the eye. "What shall I tell them?"

"That I'll join them if I can. If I can't, tell them we must attack, now. We must root them out, wherever they are, and start moving now. Tell them they may be killed now, but they surely will when dark comes."

He took her hand, then suddenly he drew her closer and kissed her lightly on the lips. "You are very lovely," he said, and was surprised to realize how true it was. "Far too lovely for this life."

She turned her back squarely on him and walked into the street. She took two steps to the outer edge of the boardwalk, where she would surely be seen by all, then she started up the street.

There was silence, then a shout. "Come back here, girl! You come right here an' you won't be hurt."

She continued to walk.

"You take another step"—the voice was harder now—"an' I'll sure enough shoot."

Ginia Blane walked on. Fallon could hear her boots on the walk.

He went to the very edge of the street. He could see her up the street . . . she was still walking.

The shot came, and the bullet kicked dirt only a few feet in front of her, but her step did not falter. And then she vanished from his sight.

He edged to the street. He saw the glint of the rifle barrel and promptly fired, holding his sight just under the rifle muzzle. The grunt of the bullet-struck man could be heard even where Fallon was, and the man's rifle fell into the street with a clatter.

In the instant after he fired, he dropped, and bullets smashed into the wall where he had stood. Running to the back of the buildings, he did not take time even to glance out, but ducked around the corner and ran for the Yankee Saloon.

He had scored three running steps before he heard the bang of the rifle and saw dirt kick in front of him. Then chips flew from a corner ahead of him and he dropped behind a water barrel and rolled out of sight just as a bullet smashed a hole in the barrel and spilled a stream of water where he had been a moment before.

His luck was running out, and he knew it. Blood had started to trickle again from his split lip. His head ached heavily. "You damn' fool!" he said to himself. "You waited too long!"

The hotel stood out from the other buildings, and it was probably from there the shots were coming. He stepped to the corner and smashed a shot into each window, then ducked and ran, bent over and trying hard for the Yankee.

He made it, slamming through the back door and bursting into the room. He slid to a stop and straightened up to see two guns on him, and half a dozen of Bellows's men, including Bellows himself. They were standing there smiling, and they had Ginia with them.

He'd bought himself a packet, and he didn't hesitate. They were grinning at him, confident, sure, and they had the drop. Only he was a gambler and a bit of a damned fool, and that they should have known. He swung the muzzle of the Henry up and opened fire as fast as he could work the lever.

He saw the confident grin on Bellows's face, the taunting smile on Semple's lips vanish in horror. At a range of twenty feet you don't miss with a rifle, and he didn't. He knew he was going to die. He felt it in every bone, but he was going to give Ginia her chance. You don't bargain with men of the Bellows type, and he knew it.

He saw Bellows jerk with the impact of his first shot. He had caught them flat-footed when he had fired instead of dropping his rifle. His was the act of a madman, but because of that very fact it came near to working— only there were too many of them.

He swung the muzzle of his rifle and let drive at Semple. Then he saw Tandy Herren suddenly step inside the door and lift his pistol, and Fallon levered two shots at him. Ginia was struggling with one of the men and she managed to lunge against another, spoiling his aim.

They were a pack of coyotes, and none of them wanted to face a rifle in that small room. Several lunged for the door at once and spilled into the street. He started toward the door, and then a heavy blow struck him and he was turned halfway around. He turned the rest of the way and saw the marksman on the gallery above him step back out of sight. He levered two shots through the floor, guessing at where he would be.

Something hit him hard in the leg, and he fell, feeling the whip of bullets past him. Ginia was fighting like a cornered wildcat with the man who had held her. Now he was only trying to get free.

Suddenly he did break loose, but she had his gun and as he scrambled for the door, she shot him.

Fallon was up on one knee. He shoved hard against the floor with his rifle stock and got up on his feet. Bellows was lying on the floor bleeding and crying for somebody to help him. Fallon stepped past him.

Ginia, her dress torn, caught at his arm, screaming, "No! no!"

He pulled away from her, fell against the door jamb, and stared stupidly into the street. The dirt of the road seemed to come alive with tiny spurts of dust, and three men lay sprawled there, dead . . . Bellows men.

He felt his knees weakening and he let go the rifle to get a better grip on the door jamb, but his fingers lacked the strength and he slid to the floor. Somebody was crying and somebody else was shooting, and far off he could hear the pound of racing hoofs. They kept pounding until their racing seemed to be inside his skull.

And then he was dead . . . or he felt like it. Never having been dead, he might have been mistaken.

———

EVIDENTLY HE WAS mistaken, for the sunshine across his bed was pleasant, and his eyes were open, looking at it. A curtain was blowing slightly with a faint breeze—but he had never had a curtain at his window.

He lay very still, afraid the curtain would go away, because he liked it and liked the feeling of lying here with nothing to worry about . . .

No, he had plenty to worry about. He had to get out of here. He had sold a claim to Pollock and the man would soon know there was no gold there, and never had been.

He turned his head slowly and saw that the room was empty. It was his room, all right, but it did not look the same. Somebody had put a rag rug on the floor, and there were curtains at all the windows, and another chair—a rocker—had been moved into the room.

He put his fingers up to feel of his eye, and then he was really worried. The swelling was gone.

If the swelling was gone he must have been lying here for days. He tried to move, but his body felt stiff. He felt of his midsection and found it was wrapped tightly in bandages. His leg, too, was bandaged.

How badly hurt was he? Could he stand the ride it would take to get out of here?

He moved himself tentatively. He was stiff, all right, but he could move. He glanced toward the door where he had left his travel gear. It was gone . . . and then he saw it, all there, even his rifle, standing just inside the closet door.

He heard a wagon in the street, the heavy rocking, rolling sound of a loaded wagon, and he listened. He heard voices . . . and down below in the saloon, somebody laughed. He had not considered the saloon. There was a way out the back, however, and he could use that.

The question was: how much time did he have?

He heard footsteps, the quick rap of light, hard heels . . . a woman walking.

Quickly, he closed his eyes, allowing one hand to lie helplessly on the blanket that covered him.

She came quickly into the room and looked down at him, then placed a hand upon his brow. It was a cool, pleasant hand. It rested for a few minutes upon his forehead, then whoever it was went to straightening the bed, which had never needed it less.

And then she seated herself in the rocker and he heard the creak of a basket, the faint click of knitting needles. After a moment, she began to sing very softly, and not at all badly. Somewhere along there, he fell asleep.

When he awakened, it was dark within the room.

No . . . not quite. There was a light across the room, shielded from his eyes.

Someone spoke . . . Brennan. "How is he?"

"He's alive." That was Ginia. Of course it would be Ginia. She was not the kind to let well enough alone. "How much alive it's hard to say." Now, that had a sarcastic tinge that his ear was delicate enough to catch.

"Pollock was asking about him. He wants to talk to him as soon as he's conscious."

Well, that was no surprise. He had ten thousand dollars of Pollock's money.

"Do you think he really intended to leave us?" Brennan asked.

"Of course. That is exactly what he would do. You saw his things . . . he was all packed to go."

"Well, he won't get away now, I'll lay a bet on that. There are some things a man never escapes. This is one of them."

"He's perfectly free."

"For how long? I tell you, he hasn't a chance, and you know it. In fact, nobody knows it better than you."

"I'm afraid you are mistaken." Her voice was stiff. "I don't know what you mean, Mr. Brennan."

"He's trapped . . . trapped, I say." Brennan did not sound too upset about it, however—and it was Brennan he had counted as a friend.

After Brennan was gone he lay perfectly still, waiting for her to go. And when she went, he would get out of here. With luck, he could be twenty miles away before daybreak . . . perhaps thirty.

Suddenly Ginia got to her feet. She put her things in the basket and closed it, then she opened a cabinet and took out a bottle. He knew the sound, all right, but it startled him and he opened his eyes.

Her back was half toward him. She had a brandy glass, and she was pouring a little from the bottle.

He closed his eyes quickly as she turned around and came toward him. "You'd better drink this," she said coolly. "You're going to need it."

He opened his eyes. "I never saw the time when I needed a drink," he said, "but I'll take it."

"You'd better," Ginia said grimly. "They'll be coming any minute now."

" 'They'?"

Her face was expressionless. "Mr. Pollock, Mr. Brennan, Joshua—all of them."

"Coming here? What for?"

"They had to make it official," she replied. And then she added, "Reverend Tattersall is coming, too."

"Reverend? In this town?"

"He's the pastor of our church. We have a church now."

He looked at her suspiciously. "How long have I been here?"

"About eight days . . . almost nine. You'd be surprised how much has happened."

He was afraid to ask what had happened. Instead he said, "How'd we come out in the fight?"

"We lost two men, and three wounded, besides you. Mr. Hamilton was killed, and Jim Karns—he was one of the new ones.

"The Bellows gang . . . they were hit pretty hard, everybody seems to think. You killed Lute Semple, Tandy Herren, and another man—we found him on the balcony—and six others were killed, most of them when you emptied the saloon."

"You mean when they busted out of the door?"

"When you started shooting and drove them out." She smiled suddenly. "They're all talking about how perfectly you had planned for them. There were four men at the mine aside from Mr. Pollock, and when those men burst out of the door they ran right into the open in front of their guns. Until then, it looked as if we'd lost the fight."

"I didn't get Bellows?"

"You wounded him. They had the trial the next day, and they tried him and another man who would never tell us his name."

"What happened?"

"They were guilty, and they were hanged. Justice is very prompt here, Mr. Fallon." And then she added slyly, "Wiley Pollock was the prosecuting attorney."

They had acted promptly then. He lay quietly thinking about it, and then he heard the boots on the steps.

"Look"—he sat up quickly, so quickly he felt a dart of pain in his side—"my horse is right down in the stable. Stall them . . . say anything . . . let me get out of here. After all," he pleaded, "I never did you any harm."

"I never let you," she said, "or you might have. After all, you did try to seduce me."

"I *what*?"

"Didn't you try to win me over with flattering words? Didn't you tell me I was too lovely for this sort of life?"

"Well, look . . . I didn't mean to . . ."

"And weren't we in a dark cellar under the hotel? How does that sound?"

Suddenly he was angry. "Look, I don't know what you're trying to do, but—"

"Oh, shut up!" she said primly. "Here they are."

John Brennan was in the lead, and behind him were Blane, Teel, Budge, Devol, Pollock, and a dozen others, some of whom he did not know.

"That claim you sold me," Pollock said, grinning, "was no damned good."

"I'm sorry about that," Fallon said. "I can return the money."

"You don't have any money," Ginia interrupted. "I used it."

"You *what?*"

"She gave it to me," Pollock said, "to develop the claim up on the mountain . . . the claim you found when you had that brush with the Utes."

"You talked when you were delirious," Ginia said maliciously, "but the claim sounded good. So I went to Mr. Pollock and suggested he go with Mr. Teel . . . he's a very good tracker, you know . . . and back-track you to where you found the gold. It took them five days to find it, but they did."

He lay perfectly still, his eyes staring out of the window. It was night out there now, and if he'd been left to himself he would be out there . . . running.

So they had located the claim *he'd* found, and she had returned *his* money to Pollock to develop the claim.

"You took the money out of my pockets? That's stealing!"

"I doubt if anybody would know more about that than you, Mr. Fallon, but time was passing and you were very ill . . . and of course, every wife has a right—"

"Every *who?*"

"Every wife. Of course, I am not your wife yet, but I told them all how you proposed to me under the hotel that time, and the things you said to me, and how we planned to be married, so Mr. Pollock and I drew up the papers for the Red Horse Mining & Development Company."

"I threw in my claim," Pollock said cheerfully, "the one you sold me."

"And we contributed ours," Ginia said, and the light in her eyes was no longer quite so malicious, "and the money you got from Mr. Pollock. You are president of the company, Mr. Pollock is vice president and superintendent of development, and I'm the treasurer."

"And we had an election," Blane interrupted, "and you were elected mayor. I voted against you," he added.

"You're the only sane one in the crowd," Fallon said irritably. "This has turned into a madhouse."

"And this," Ginia said, indicating a man standing near her, "is the Reverend Mr. Tattersall."

The door opened just then and Joshua Teel's wife came in with a cake, followed by Ruth Damon, in her prettiest dress.

"What's that for?" Fallon asked.

"That's the wedding cake, Mr. Fallon," Ginia replied, "and Ruth is my bridesmaid."

"This has gone far enough!" Fallon protested. "A joke is a joke. I never proposed to you—never!"

"Not in so many words," Ginia agreed.

"How many do?" Mrs. Teel asked. "In so many words? Josh didn't."

"Neither did Pa," Mrs. Blane said, "not in so many words."

The Reverend Mr. Tattersall came up beside the bed. He cleared his throat.

"We wouldn't like to have it said," Riordan commented, "that one of our girls was slighted. Why, I've seen men hung for less."

The Reverend Mr. Tattersall cleared his throat again, more emphatically. "We are gathered here . . ."

Macon Fallon was no stranger to the town of Red Horse, and the fact that he was a man with a fast horse wasn't going to do him a damned bit of good.

WHAT IS LOUIS L'AMOUR'S
LOST TREASURES?

L ouis L'Amour's Lost Treasures is a project created to release some of the author's more unconventional manuscripts from the family archives.

Currently included in the project are *Louis L'Amour's Lost Treasures: Volume 1,* published in the fall of 2017, and *Volume 2,* which will be published in the fall of 2019. These books contain both finished and unfinished short stories, unfinished novels, literary and motion picture treatments, notes, and outlines. They are a wide selection of the many works Louis was never able to publish during his lifetime.

In 2018 we released *No Traveller Returns,* L'Amour's never-before-seen first novel, which was written between 1938 and 1942. In the future, there may be a selection of even more L'Amour titles.

Additionally, many notes and alternate drafts to Louis's well-known and previously published novels and short stories will now be included as "bonus feature" postscripts within the books that they relate to. For example, the Lost Treasures postscript to *Last of the Breed* will contain early notes on the story, the short story that was discovered to be a missing piece of the novel, the history of the novel's inspiration and creation, and information about unproduced motion picture and comic book versions.

An even more complete description of the Lost Treasures project, along with a number of examples of what is in the books, can be found at louislamourslosttreasures .com. The website also contains a good deal of exclusive material, such as even more pieces of unknown stories that were too short or too incomplete to include in the Lost Treasures books, plus personal photos, scans of original documents, and notes.

All of the works that contain Lost Treasures project materials will display the Louis L'Amour's Lost Treasures banner and logo.

LOUIS L'AMOUR'S LOST TREASURES

POSTSCRIPT

By Beau L'Amour

Of my father's many novels, *Fallon* is one of my favorites. I love that Macon Fallon is not your typical hero. He's more like Harold Hill in *The Music Man,* a con man who, despite his ill intentions, ends up helping the people he is trying to take advantage of. More lighthearted than some of his other novels, in *Fallon* I can feel the fun Dad was having when he wrote the book.

Besides the playful use of prose, *Fallon* indulges in other whimsical details, like the names on many of the shop signs on the Buell's Bluff street. They all refer to my mother's friends and family: Susan Brown's Hats was named after longtime *General Hospital* star Susan Brown, a friend of Mom's from her days at USC. The Veitch Hotel relates to John Veitch, an executive production manager at Columbia Pictures, who was married to Carol Lee Ladd, stepdaughter of movie star Alan Ladd and my mother's oldest friend. Deming's Emporium was named for another of Mom's friends, Millicent Deming, and Pearly Gates' Saloon is a spoof on Phyllis Gates, briefly the wife of Rock Hudson. Mom Jelks is most definitely a nod to my great-grandmother, Belle Jelks.

Here is an early, alternate beginning to the novel. It

moves slightly faster than the final version and contains some additional history and characters:

CHAPTER ONE

Macon Fallon was a drifting man. He was also, at the moment, a man without money. To a man without money his problems are simple indeed. He must get money.

The nearest advisable settlement was a hundred miles west, and the nearest inadvisable settlement was somewhat less than that distance to the east. The hospitality of that settlement had ceased abruptly and the population had escorted Fallon out of town. However, he had been discreet enough to start with a substantial lead, so the rope they carried went unused.

There had been a minor altercation over two fours Fallon had drawn to fill out his hand. To at least one gambler the drawing of fours seemed too opportune to be accidental and led to the drawing of sixes. The local citizen lost that draw also. However, he was a popular citizen and Macon Fallon was a stranger.

Keenly sensitive to the temper of crowds, Macon Fallon was not only a

stranger. He was a stranger with a
fast horse.

He wasted no time gathering up the
money, perfectly aware that life
without money was possible, money
without life, impossible.

He had been two days without food
when he saw the wagons, and several
hours without water.

Obviously, from the way the first
wagon was canted to one side, it had
a broken wheel, and as he drew
closer he could see their stock was
in bad shape. The oxen and horses
were gaunt, the people themselves
drawn and tired. There were two men,
two women of mature years, a boy of
sixteen or so, two young and pretty
girls, and three smaller children.

Macon Fallon was a cynic, but
every cynic is a sentimentalist
under the skin, and therein lay the
chink in his armor of larceny. Aware
of this, he avoided every contact
that might betray him into
thoughtfulness and consideration.
People, he told himself, were
suckers. The fact that he himself on
occasion had been a sucker served
only to prove his point.

Aware of his softness, Macon
Fallon chose to deal with only the

most ruthless, relentless, and self-seeking. Because of this his conscience rarely suffered.

Two assets had Macon Fallon aside from his glib tongue--the first a keen sense of observation, the second a mind filled to the over-flowing with an enormous variety of apparently useless information. As to observation, Fallon had noticed that while all people look, few really *see*. Therefore he had trained himself to notice, to observe quickly but miss nothing . . . as he did not now miss the sign.

It lay among a mass of tumbleweed beside the trail, forgotten, almost weathered out of existence.

Buell's Bluff . . . *Buell's Bluff*!

Macon Fallon stiffened, and sat straight in the saddle, cocking his flat-brimmed, flat-crowned hat at a jauntier angle.

He swept off his hat. "May I be of service?" His observant eye caught the glimmer of a fire, his nostrils caught the aroma of coffee and a fragrance that could be nothing but frying bacon. His stomach growled an angry warning that it would put up with this nonsense no longer. "You seem to be in some kind of trouble."

"Wheel broke." The bigger man

walked over to him. "We haven't the tools to fix it."

Macon Fallon swung down from the saddle and dusted his clothes with his hat. "You were going to the mines?" he asked politely.

"Figured to," the other man said. "Not much chance of us making it unless we leave our wagons and strike out afoot." He glanced at the heat-shimmering desert that lay ahead and to the south. "Kind of scared to try that."

"Rightly so, sir, rightly so." Fallon glanced at the girls. One of them—he averted his eyes quickly. No time for sentimentality. These were good people, the kind he usually avoided, but this was neither the time nor the place for sentiment. Anyway, he was not planning to victimize them . . . well not exactly . . . just to *use* them. Their assistance and presence, at least.

He allowed himself a wide, friendly smile. "Believe me, folks, your wheel chose the right place to break down. There's no reason to go further. Have you heard"—he paused, and his eyes fell on the sorrel horse tied to the tail-gate of the wagon—"of the town of Red Horse?"

They had not, but he expected that. Until a moment before he had not heard of it, either.

"Red Horse," he said, "was a mining town, born right out of the desert, and it started to be the richest strike among the mines. My uncle Joe, God rest his soul, was among the founders and the owner of the richest claims. Then the Piutes struck. They came suddenly, in the night, and every man-jack of the settlers wiped out. Killed . . . slaughtered."

He paused, glancing over the group that stood around him, open-mouthed. All but that girl, who looked at him with level eyes, direct, sincere, and discerning . . . altogether too discerning.

"The town was lost. Nobody knew where it was; the claims were forgotten. It hadn't the time to become widely known, and all who really knew where it was were dead. Only one thing kept it from being forever lost."

"What was that?"

He had their attention all right. They had forgotten their troubles, gripped by his story. It was not so much what he was saying as what their imaginations were doing to his story. "There was a letter," he said. "My uncle wrote a letter." He placed a hand to his breast. "I have it . . . here."

"All very well, mister," the first man objected, "but what's that got to do with us?"

Fallon smiled. "Do I smell coffee? And bacon? Perhaps we could discuss this further over our coffee?"

It had taken him no longer to evolve his plan, but a glance or two told him these were not the lambs to be fleeced. Quite obviously they were lacking in fleece, and all that remained to them was their substantial supplies, their worn-out oxen, tired horses, and some remnant of hope.

Hope they needed, however, for what they retained was thin, flimsy, exhausted by heat, dust, and miles. There was no hope in the name of Buell's Bluff . . . a singular lack of it, in fact. So he'd invented the name of Red Horse.

What's in a name? A town by any other name can be as big a fraud.

Their wagons had stopped, he told them, at an opportune time, for to have the gold they wanted, the land they wanted, the businesses they might want, they need go no further.

He was the Moses who could lead them
to the promised land . . . the
papers were drawn up.

Red Horse had been abandoned for
years. They would all pitch in,
rebuild, sweep out, and brush up.
They would put their remaining stock
of provisions on the market, sell
them for extortionate prices . . .
he did not use the adjective . . .
and they would be in partnership.

They were, he assured them, free
to take up claims so long as they
remained away from his own, but the
real money might come from business.
Men had to eat, sleep, and use
tools, wear clothing even if they
found no gold. They would outfit the
businesses, handle the sales, and
he would take thirty percent. Of the
gold claims he would take only ten
percent for guiding them to the
area, advice, assistance, etc.

"Is there gold there?" Tom Blaine
asked.

"My uncle said it was the biggest
strike he had ever seen"--all the
gold his uncle had seen was in his
wedding ring--"but I can promise
nothing."

"The point is," he said
confidentially, "we wouldn't have to
find gold to make money. We'll be

located just off the main migration
route at an intermediate point
between towns . . . we're sure to
do business."

"There'll have to be a saloon,"
Carter grumbled, "and I don't hold
with whiskey drinking."

"Leave that to me," Fallon
suggested dryly, "what they get
won't be whiskey."

With all the remaining oxen
hitched to the one good wagon and
young Tom Blaine left to guard the
wagon with the broken wheel, they
made their start. Once they arrived
in Red Horse they could dismount a
good wheel from this wagon and send
back for the other.

Macon Fallon was ashamed when
he saw the hope in their faces,
the sudden enthusiasm now that a
decision had been made and they were
near a destination. He rode off in
the lead, but had gone only a short
distance when Ginia Blaine rode up
beside him.

She was pretty, no getting around
that, and she had a disturbing
figure, but it was her eyes that
worried him. She might be young, but
Ginia Blaine had a cool, level way
of looking at a man that seemed to

see through all the blarney and soft soap he could hand out.

"Mr. Fallon"--Ginia was not one to beat around the chaparral-- "is this a wild goose chase?"

Macon Fallon blushed, and hurriedly mopped his face with a handkerchief to cover his embarrassment. Buell's Bluff had been a fraud, a gold-rush hurriedly promoted by a group of confidence men using salted claims, but before it was discovered men had thronged in, built stores and opened a bank. The bottom had fallen out with a thud so loud they had even heard about it back east. It had been written about in Boston, New York, and even in London.

That had been seven years ago, and so far as Fallon was aware nobody had been near the place since.

"Gold is where you find it," Macon Fallon replied, with great originality, "and a man never knows. It was *said* to be a big strike"--he was on safe ground there--"but the town was deserted after the Piutes attacked."

There was even truth in that. The last nine people at Buell's Bluff had been wiped out by Piutes.

"I don't trust you, Mr. Fallon,"

Ginia replied coolly. "If you take advantage of us, you'll be sorry. I'll find a way to make you sorry."

He had been watching the trail. There were no tracks, either coming or going, nor any sign of recent travel at all. They wound up the old trail to the top of the ridge, taking time out to roll a few rocks out of the way, and started down the opposite side. The town lay only two miles ahead but was safely and securely hidden, situated on the bench above a frequently dry stream bed, but concealed by hills that withheld all view until one was actually inside the canyon itself.

The town was there. Neither time nor dust or fire had blotted it out. Macon Fallon, following the flickering torch of fortune, had pursued it once before to this place. He had never been far behind any boom, and he had come into this one among the first, and had been among the last to leave. Pursuing the will o' wisp of luck at the gaming tables instead of the pan and rocker, he had done rather well at Buell's Bluff until, leaving town, he had been brutally and abruptly robbed of all he owned by one Red Chase.

The fact was, Macon had been the last to leave . . . awakening in bed after a bad night to find the town deserted, only a coffee pot left on the stove, and a couple of eggs and some bacon beside it. Coffee Bob Buell had not had the heart to leave him totally without breakfast, so when the town deserted, Coffee Bob left behind the makings.

It was after breakfast, with light heart and heavy pockets, Macon Fallon had started from town. Red Chase had been awaiting him beside the trail.

Hours later Macon Fallon was walking and his wallet was empty. He had a knot on his head and a carefully stored memory of Red Chase, whom he had briefly glimpsed as he tumbled into oblivion.

All this returned to him as he saw the town. A brief canter through the street told him nothing was changed. The mirror behind the bar was unbroken, the glasses stood in neat if dusty rows, the tools had remained where they had been left in the blacksmith shop.

Two days later, the town of Red Horse was ready for customers. The saloon had been swept out, the glasses polished, and the bakery

down the street, in the capable
hands of Ma Carter, was baking . . .
on the advice of Fallon . . .
doughnuts. Or as they were known in
the West . . . bear sign.

The supply store had been opened
with what extra provisions could be
spared from the two wagons, on sale
at three times the usual prices.
The blacksmith shop was ready for
business, and Macon Fallon had
ridden back to the main route of the
covered wagons to put up a
sign . . . and to carefully break up
and discard the old BUELL'S BLUFF
sign he had seen earlier.

He had just completed this
destruction when he glanced around
and saw Pop Foster watching him. The
old prospector grinned. "Red Horse,
hey? Good a name as any. What you
got in mind, Macon? Ain't no gold up
there, an' you know it."

"Where'd you come from, you old
horse-thief?"

"Horse-thief? Never stole a horse
in my life . . . cows, maybe, but
no horses." Pop Foster moved closer.
"Look here, boy, what ever it is
you're fixin' to do, I could help. I
really could!"

"Who says I need help?"

"You'll need it. Red Chase is back

```
in the hills. He's back there and
he's got six or seven of the meanest
outlaws you ever did see. If I
remember right, you an' Red didn't
take to each other."
```

There are a few details lurking in this first draft that I wish had made it into the novel, but that was Dad— he might occasionally rewrite, or restart, a story, but it was rare for him to do much analysis of the assets and liabilities of his various drafts. The newest one was always the best, in his mind.

My father actually wrote two stories about the fictional town of Red Horse and its problems with confidence men. Though "Elisha Comes to Red Horse" is sort of a sequel, I believe Dad actually conceived of it before Fallon. Louis toyed briefly with the idea of expanding it into a novel in the mid-1970s, and at some point had hopes that he would be able to turn "Elisha" into a Broadway musical. Dad always loved the theater, and even invested in a show or two in the late 1950s. It was finally published in the collection *End of the Drive* in 1997.

Elisha Comes to Red Horse

```
   There is a new church in the town
of Red Horse. A clean white church
of board and bat with a stained-
glass window, a tall pointed
steeple, and a bell that we've
been told came all the way from
Youngstown, Ohio. Nearby is a
```

comfortable parsonage, a two-story
house with a garreted roof, and
fancy gingerbread under the eaves.

Just down the hill from the church
and across from the tailings of
what was once the King James Mine
is a carefully kept cemetery of
white headstones and neatly fitted
crosses. It is surrounded by a
spiked iron fence six feet high,
and the gate is always fastened with
a heavy lock. We open it up only for
funerals and when the groundskeeper
makes his rounds. Outsiders standing
at the barred gate may find that a
bit odd . . . but the people of Red
Horse wouldn't have it any other
way.

Visitors come from as far away as
Virginia City to see our church, and
on Sundays when we pass the
collection, why, quite a few of
those strangers ante up with the
rest of us. Now Red Horse has seen
its times of boom and bust and our
history is as rough as any other
town in the West, but our new church
has certainly become the pride of
the county.

And it is all thanks to the man
that we called Brother Elisha.

He was six feet five inches tall
and he came into town a few years

ago riding the afternoon stage. He wore a black broadcloth frock coat and carried a small valise. He stepped down from the stage, swept off his tall black hat, spread his arms, and lifted his eyes to the snowcapped ridges beyond the town. When he had won every eye on the street he said, "I come to bring deliverance, and eternal life!"

And then he crossed the street to the hotel, leaving the sound of his magnificent voice echoing against the false-fronted, unpainted buildings of our street.

In our town we've had our share of the odd ones, and many of the finest and best, but this was something new in Red Horse.

"A sky pilot, Marshal." Ralston spat into the dust. "We got ourselves another durned sky pilot!"

"It's a cinch he's no cattleman," I said, "and he doesn't size up like a drummer."

"We've got a sky pilot," Brace grumbled, "and one preacher ought to balance off six saloons, so we sure don't need another."

"I say he's a gambler," Brennen argued. "That was just a grandstand play. Red Horse attracts gamblers like manure attracts flies. First time he gets in a game he'll cold deck you in the most sanctified way you ever did see!"

At daybreak the stranger walked up the mountain. Years ago lightning had struck the base of the ridge, and before rain put out the fire it burned its way up the mountain in a wide avenue. Strangely, nothing had ever again grown on that slope. Truth to tell, we'd had some mighty dry years after that, and nothing much had grown anywhere.

The Utes were superstitious about it. They said the lightning had put a curse on the mountain, but we folks in Red Horse put no faith in that. Or not much.

It was almighty steep to the top of that ridge, and every step the stranger took was in plain sight of the town, but he walked out on that spring morning and strode down the street and up the mountain. Those long legs of his took him up like he was walking a graded road, and when he got to the flat rock atop the butte he turned back toward the town and lifted his arms to the heavens.

"He's prayin'," Ralston said, studying him through Brennen's glass. "He's sure enough prayin'!"

"I maintain he's a gambler,"

Brennen insisted. "Why can't he do his praying in church like other folks? Ask the reverend and see what he says."

Right then the reverend came out of the Emporium with a small sack of groceries under his arm, and noting the size of the sack, I felt like ducking into Brennen's Saloon. When prosperity and good weather come to Red Horse, we're inclined to forget our preacher and sort of stave off the doctor bills, too. Only in times of drought or low-grade ore do we attend church regular and support the preacher as we ought.

"What do you make of him, Preacher?" Brace asked.

The reverend squinted his eyes at the tiny figure high upon the hill. "There are many roads to grace," he said. "Perhaps he has found his."

"If he's a preacher, why don't he pray in church?" Brennen protested.

"The groves were God's first temples," the reverend quoted. "There's no need to pray in church. A prayer offered up anywhere is heard by the Lord."

Ralston went into the hotel, and we followed him in to see what name the man had used. It was written

plain as print: Brother Elisha,
Damascus.

We stood back and looked at each
other. We'd never had anybody in
Red Horse from Damascus. We'd never
had anybody from farther away than
Denver except maybe a drummer who
claimed he'd been to St. Louis . . .
but we never believed him.

It was nightfall before Brother
Elisha came down off the mountain,
and he went at once to the hotel.
Next day Brace came up to Brennen
and me. "You know, I was talking to
Sampson. He says he's never even
seen Brother Elisha yet."

"What of it?" Brennen says. "I
still say he's a gambler."

"If he don't eat at Sampson's"--
Brace paused for emphasis--"where
does he eat?"

We stared at each other. Most of
us had our homes and wives to cook
for us, some of the others batched
it, but stoppers-by or ones who
didn't favor their own cooking, they
ate at Sampson's. There just wasn't
anywhere else to eat.

"There he goes now," Brennen said,
"looking sanctimonious as a dog
caught in his own hen coop."

"Now see here!" Ralston protested.
"Don't be talking that way, Brennen.

After all, we don't know who he
might be!"

Brother Elisha passed us by like a
pay-car passes a tramp, and turning
at the corner he started up the
mountain. It was a good two miles up
that mountain and the man climbed
two thousand feet or more, with no
switchbacks or twist-arounds, but he
walked right up it. I wouldn't say
that was a steep climb, but it
wasn't exactly a promenade, either.

Brace scratched his jaw. "Maybe
the man's broke," he suggested. "We
can't let a man of God starve right
here amongst us. What would the
folks in Virginia City say?"

"Who says he's a man of God?"
Brennen was always irreverent. "Just
because he wears a black suit and
goes up a mountain to pray?"

"It won't do," Brace insisted, "to
have it said a preacher starved
right here in Red Horse."

"The reverend," I suggested,
"might offer some pointers on that."

They ignored me, looking mighty
stiff and self-important.

"We could take up a collection,"
Ralston suggested.

Brother Elisha had sure stirred up
a sight of conversation around town,
but nobody knew anything because he

hadn't said two words to anybody.
The boys at the hotel, who have a
way of knowing such things, said he
hadn't nothing in his valise but two
shirts, some underwear, and a Bible.

That night there was rain. It was
a soft, pleasant spring rain, the
kind we call a growing rain, and it
broke a two-year dry spell. Whenever
we get a rain like that we know that
spring has surely come, for they are
warm rains and they melt the snow
from the mountains and start the
seeds germinating again. The snow
gone from the ridges is the first
thing we notice after such a rain,
but next morning it wasn't only the
snow, for something else had
happened. Up that long-dead hillside
where Brother Elisha walked, there
was a faint mist of green, like the
first sign of growing grass.

Brace came out, then Ralston and
some others, and we stood looking up
the mountain. No question about it,
the grass was growing where no grass
had grown in years. We stared up at
it with a kind of awe and wondering.

"It's him!" Brace spoke in a low,
shocked voice. "Brother Elisha has
done this."

"Have you gone off your head?"
Brennen demanded irritably. "This is

just the first good growing weather we've had since the fire. The last few years there's been little rain, and that late, and the ground has been cold right into the summer."

"You believe what you want," Ralston said. "We know what we can see. The Utes knew that hillside was accursed, but now he's walked on it, the curse is lifted. He said he would bring life, and he has."

It was all over town. Several times folks tried to get into talk with Brother Elisha, but he merely lifted a hand as if blessing them and went his way. But each time he came down from the mountain, his cheeks were flushed with joy and his eyes were glazed like he'd been looking into the eternity of heaven.

All this time nothing was heard from Reverend Sanderson, so what he thought about Brother Elisha, nobody knew. Here and there we began to hear talk that he was the new Messiah, but nobody seemed to pay much mind to that talk. Only it made a man right uneasy . . . how was one expected to act toward a Messiah?

In Red Horse we weren't used to distinguished visitors. It was out of the way, back in the hills, off the main roads east and west. Nobody ever came to Red Horse, unless they were coming to Red Horse.

Brennen had stopped talking. One time after he'd said something sarcastic it looked like he might be mobbed, so he kept his mouth shut, and I was just as satisfied, although it didn't seem to me that he'd changed his opinion of Brother Elisha. He always was a stubborn cuss.

Now personally, I didn't cater to this Messiah talk. There was a time or two when I had the sneaking idea that maybe Brennen knew what he was talking about, but I sure enough didn't say it out loud. Most people in Red Horse were kind of proud of Brother Elisha even when he made them uncomfortable. Mostly I'm a man likes a hand of poker now and again, and I'm not shy about a bottle, although not likely to get all liquored up. On the other hand, I rarely miss a Sunday at meeting unless the fishing is awful good, and I contribute. Maybe not as much as I could, but I contribute.

The reverend was an understanding sort of man, but about this here Brother Elisha, I wasn't sure. So I shied away from him on the street, but come Sunday I was in church.

Only a half dozen were there. That was the day Brother Elisha held his first meeting.

There must've been three hundred people out there on that green mountainside when Brother Elisha called his flock together. Nobody knew how the word got around, but suddenly everybody was talking about it and most of them went out of curiosity.

By all accounts Brother Elisha turned out to be a Hell-and-damnation preacher with fire and thunder in his voice, and even there in the meeting house while the reverend talked we could hear those mighty tones rolling up against the rock walls of the mountains and sounding in the canyons as Brother Elisha called on the Lord to forgive the sinners on the Great Day coming.

Following Sunday I was in church again, but there was nobody there but old Ansel Greene's widow who mumbled to herself and never knew which side was up . . . except about money. The old woman had it, but hadn't spent enough to fill a coffee can since old Ansel passed on.

Just the two of us were there, and the reverend looked mighty down in the mouth, but nonetheless he got up

in the pulpit and looked down at
those rows of empty seats and
announced a hymn.

Now I am one of these here folks
who don't sing. Usually when hymns
are sung I hang on to a hymnal with
both hands and shape the words and
rock my head to the tune, but I
don't let any sound come out. But
this time there was no chance of
that. It was up to me to sing or get
off the spot, and I sang. The
surprise came when right behind me a
rich baritone rolled out, and when I
turned to look, it was Brennen.

Unless you knew Brennen this
wouldn't mean much. Once an
Orangeman, Brennen was an avowed and
argumentative atheist. Nothing he
liked better than an argument about
the Bible, and he knew more about it
than most preachers, but he scoffed
at it. Since the reverend had been
in town his one great desire had
been to get Brennen into church, but
Brennen just laughed at him,
although like all of us he both
liked and respected the reverend.

So here was Brennen, giving voice
there back of me, and I doubt if the
reverend would have been as pleased
had the church been packed. Brennen
sang, no nonsense about it, and when

the responses were read, he spoke out strong and sure.

At the door the reverend shook hands with him. "It is a pleasure to have you with us, Brother Brennen."

"It's a pleasure to be here, Reverend," Brennen said. "I may not always agree with you, Parson, but you're a good man, a very good man. You can expect me next Sunday, sir."

Walking up the street, Brennen said, "My ideas haven't changed, but Sanderson is a decent man, entitled to a decent attendance at his church, and his congregation should be ashamed. Ashamed, I say!"

Brennen was alone in his saloon next day. Brother Elisha had given an impassioned sermon on the sinfulness of man and the coming of the Great Day, and he scared them all hollow.

You never saw such a changed town. Ralston, who spoke only two languages, American and profane, was suddenly talking like a Baptist minister at a Bible conference and looking so sanctimonious it would fair turn a man's stomach.

Since Brother Elisha started preaching, the two emptiest places in town were the church and the saloon. Nor would I have you thinking wrong of the saloon. In my day in the West, a saloon was a club, a meeting place, a forum, and a source of news all put together. It was the only place men could gather to exchange ideas, do business, or hear the latest news from the outside.

And every day Brother Elisha went up the mountain.

One day when I stopped by the saloon, Brennen was outside watching Brother Elisha through his field glasses.

"Is he prayin'?" I asked.

"You might say. He lifts his arms to the sky, rants around some, then he disappears over the hill. Then he comes back and rants around some more and comes down the hill."

"I suppose he has to rest," I said. "Prayin' like that can use up a sight of energy."

"I suppose so," he said doubtfully. After a moment or two, he asked, "By the way, Marshal, were you ever in Mobeetie?"

By that time most of that great blank space on the mountainside had grown up to grass, and it grew greenest and thickest right where Brother Elisha walked, and that caused more talk.

Not in all this time had Brother Elisha been seen to take on any nourishment, not a bite of anything, nor to drink, except water from the well.

When Sunday came around again the only two in church were Brennen and me, but Brennen was there, all slicked up mighty like a winning gambler, and when the reverend's wife passed the plate, Brennen dropped in a twenty-dollar gold piece. Also, I'd heard he'd had a big package of groceries delivered around to the one-room log parsonage.

The town was talking of nothing but Brother Elisha, and it was getting so a man couldn't breathe the air around there, it was so filled with sanctified hypocrisy. You never saw such a bunch of overnight gospel-shouters.

Now I can't claim to be what you'd call a religious man, yet I've a respect for religion, and when a man lives out his life under the sun and the stars, half the time riding alone over mountains and desert, then he usually has a religion although it may not be the usual variety. Moreover, I had a respect for the reverend.

Brennen had his say about Brother Elisha, but I never did, although there was something about him that didn't quite tally.

Then the miracle happened.

It was a Saturday morning and Ed Colvin was shingling the new livery barn, and in a town the size of Red Horse nobody could get away from the sound of that hammer, not that we cared, or minded the sound. Only it was always with us.

And then suddenly we didn't hear it anymore.

Now it wasn't noontime, and Ed was a working sort of man, as we'd discovered in the two months he'd been in town. It was not likely he'd be quitting so early.

"Gone after lumber," I suggested.

"He told me this morning," Brace said, "that he had enough laid by to last him two days. He was way behind and didn't figure on quitting until lunchtime."

"Wait," I said, "we'll hear it again."

Only when some time passed and we heard nothing we started for the barn. Ed had been working mighty close to the peak of what was an unusually steep roof.

We found him lying on the ground

and there was blood on his head and we sent for the doc.

Now Doc McDonald ain't the greatest doctor, but he was all we had aside from the midwife and a squaw up in the hills who knew herbs. The doc was drunk most of the time these days and showing up with plenty of money, so's it had been weeks since he'd been sober.

Doc came over, just weaving a mite, and almost as steady as he usually is when sober. He knelt by Ed Colvin and looked him over. He listened for a heartbeat and he held a mirror over his mouth, and he got up and brushed off his knees. "What's all the rush for? This man is dead!"

We carried him to Doc's place, Doc being the undertaker, too, and we laid him out on the table in his back room. Ed's face was dead white except for the blood, and he stared unblinking until the doc closed his eyes.

We walked back to the saloon feeling low. We'd not known Ed too well, but he was a quiet man and a good worker, and we needed such men around our town. Seemed a shame for him to go when there were others,

mentioning no names, who meant less
to the town.

That was the way it was until
Brother Elisha came down off the
mountain. He came with long strides,
staring straight before him, his
face flushed with the happiness that
seemed always with him these days.
He was abreast of the saloon when he
suddenly stopped.

It was the first time he had ever
stopped to speak to anyone, aside
from his preaching.

"What has happened?" he asked. "I
miss the sound of the hammer. The
sounds of labor are blessed in the
ears of the Lord."

"Colvin fell," Brace said. "He
fell from the roof and was killed."

Brother Elisha looked at him out
of his great dark eyes and he said,
"There is no death. None pass on but
for the Glory of the Lord, and I
feel this one passed before his
time."

"You may think there's no death,"
Brace said, "but Ed Colvin looks
mighty dead to me."

He turned his eyes on Brace. "O, ye
of little faith: Take me to him."

When we came into Doc McDonald's
the air was foul with liquor, and
Brace glared at Doc like he'd

committed a blasphemy. Brother Elisha paused briefly, his nose twitching, and then he walked through to the back room where Ed Colvin lay.

We paused at the door, clustered there, not knowing what to expect, but Brother Elisha walked up and bowed his head, placing the palm of his right hand on Colvin's brow, and then he prayed. Never did I know a man who could make a prayer fill a room with sound like Brother Elisha, but there at the last he took Ed by the shoulders and he pulled him into a sitting position and he said, "Edward Colvin, your work upon this earth remains unfinished. For the Glory of the Lord . . . rise!"

And I'll be forever damned if Ed Colvin didn't take a long gasping breath and sit right up on that table. He looked mighty confused and Brother Elisha whispered in his ear for a moment and then with a murmur of thanks Ed Colvin got up and walked right out of the place.

We stood there like we'd been petrified, and I don't know what we'd been expecting, but it wasn't this. Brother Elisha said, "The Lord moves in mysterious ways His wonders to perform." And then he left us.

Brace looked at me and I looked at Ralston and when I started to speak my mouth was dry. And just then we heard the sound of a hammer.

When I went outside people were filing into the street and they were looking up at that barn, staring at Ed Colvin, working away as if nothing had happened. When I passed Damon, standing in the bank door, his eyes were wide open and his face white. I spoke to him but he never even heard me or saw me. He was just standing there staring at Colvin.

By nightfall everybody in town was whispering about it, and when Sunday morning came they flocked to hear him preach, their faces shining, their eyes bright as though with fever.

When the reverend stepped into the pulpit, Brennen was the only one there besides me.

Reverend Sanderson looked stricken, and that morning he talked in a low voice, speaking quietly and sincerely but lacking his usual force. "Perhaps," he said as we left, "perhaps it is we who are wrong. The Lord gives the power of miracles to but few."

"There are many kinds of miracles," Brennen replied, "and one miracle is to find a sane, solid man in a town that's running after a red wagon."

As the three of us walked up the street together we heard the great rolling voice of Brother Elisha: "And I say unto you that the gift of life to Brother Colvin was but a sign, for on the morning of the coming Sabbath we shall go hence to the last resting place of your loved ones, and there I shall cause them all to be raised, and they shall live again, and take their places among you as of old!"

You could have dropped a feather. We stood on the street in back of his congregation and we heard what he said, but we didn't believe it, we couldn't believe it.

He was going to bring back the dead.

Brother Elisha, who had brought Ed Colvin back to life, was now going to empty the cemetery, returning to life all those who had passed on . . . and some who had been helped.

"The Great Day has come!" He lifted his long arms and spread them wide, and his sonorous voice rolled against the mountains. "And men shall live again for the Glory of

All Highest! Your wives, your mothers, your brothers and fathers, they shall walk beside you again!"

And then he led them into the singing of a hymn and the three of us walked away.

That was the quietest Sunday Red Horse ever knew. Not a whisper, all day long. Folks were scared, they were happy, they were inspired. The townsfolk walked as if under a spell.

Strangely, it was Ed Colvin who said it. Colvin, the man who had gone to the great beyond and returned . . . although he claimed he had no memory of anything after his fall.

Brace was talking about the joy of seeing his wife again, and Ed said quietly, "You'll also be seeing your mother-in-law."

Brace's mouth opened and closed twice before he could say anything at all, and then he didn't want to talk. He stood there like somebody had exploded a charge of powder under his nose, and then he turned sharply around and walked off.

"I've got more reason than any of you to be thankful," Ed said, his eyes downcast. "But I'm just not sure this is all for the best."

We all glanced at each other. "Think about it." Ed got up, looking kind of embarrassed. "What about you, Ralston? You'll have to go back to work. Do you think your uncle will stand for you loafing and spending the money he worked so hard to get?"

"That's right," I agreed, "you'll have to give it all back."

Ralston got mad. He started to shout that he wouldn't do any such thing, and anyway, if his uncle came back now he would be a changed man, he wouldn't care for money any longer, he--

"You don't believe that," Brennen said. "You know darned well that uncle of yours was the meanest skinflint in this part of the country. Nothing would change him."

Ralston went away from there. Seemed to me he wanted to do some thinking.

When I turned to leave, Brennen said, "Where are you going?"

"Well," I said, "seems to me I'd better oil up my six-shooters. There's three men in that Boot Hill that I put there. Looks like I'll have it to do over."

He laughed. "You aren't falling for this, are you?"

"Colvin sounds mighty lively to me," I said, "and come Sunday morning Brother Elisha has got to put up or shut up."

"You don't believe that their time in the hereafter will have changed those men you killed."

"Brennen," I said, "if I know the Hame brothers, they'll come out of their graves like they went into them. They'll come a-shootin'."

There had been no stage for several days as the trail had been washed out by a flash flood, and the town was quiet and it was scared. Completely cut off from the outside, all folks could do was wait and get more and more frightened as the Great Day approached. At first everybody had been filled with happiness at the thought of the dead coming back, and then suddenly, like Brace and Ralston, everybody was taking another thought.

There was the Widow McCann who had buried three husbands out there, all of them fighters and all of them mean. There were a dozen others with reason to give the matter some thought, and I knew at least two who were packed and waiting for the first stage out of town.

Brace dropped in at the saloon for

his first drink since Brother Elisha started to preach. He hadn't shaved and he looked mighty mean. "Why'd he pick on this town?" he burst out. "When folks are dead they should be left alone. Nobody has a right to interfere with nature thataway."

Brennen mopped his bar, saying nothing at all.

Ed Colvin dropped around. "Wish that stage would start running. I want to leave town. Folks treat me like I was some kind of freak."

"Stick around," Brennen said. "Come Sunday the town will be filled with folks like you. A good carpenter will be able to stay busy, so busy he won't care what folks say about him. Take Streeter there. He'll need a new house now that his brother will be wanting his house back."

Streeter slammed his glass on the bar. "All right, damn it!" he shouted angrily. "I'll build my own house!"

Ralston motioned to me and we walked outside. Brace was there, and Streeter joined us. "Look," Ralston whispered, "Brace and me, we've talked it over. Maybe if we were to talk to Brother Elisha . . . maybe he'd call the whole thing off."

"Are you crazy?" I asked.

His eyes grew mean. "You want to try those Hame boys again? Seems to me you came out mighty lucky the last time. How do you know you'll be so lucky again? Those boys were pure-dee poison."

That was gospel truth, but I stood there chewing my cigar a minute and then said, "No chance. He wouldn't listen to us."

Ed Colvin had come up. "A man doing good works," he said, "might be able to use a bit of money. Although I suppose it would take quite a lot."

Brace stood a little straighter but when he turned to Colvin, the carpenter was hurrying off down the street. When I turned around there was Brennen leaning on the doorjamb, and he was smiling.

Friday night when I was making my rounds I saw somebody slipping up the back stairs of the hotel, and for a moment his face was in the light from a window. It was Brace.

Later, I saw Ralston hurrying home from the direction of the hotel, and you'd be surprised at some of the folks I spotted slipping up those back stairs to commune with Brother

Elisha. Even Streeter, and even Damon.

Watching Damon come down those back stairs I heard a sound behind me and turned to see Brennen standing there in the dark. "Seems a lot of folks are starting to think this resurrection of the dead isn't an unmixed blessing."

"You know something?" I said thoughtfully. "Nobody has been atop that hill since Brother Elisha started his walks. I think I'll just meander up there and have a look around."

"You've surprised me," Brennen said. "I wouldn't have expected you to be a churchgoing man. You're accustomed to sinful ways."

"Why, now," I said, "when I come into a town to live, I go to church. If the preacher is a man who shouts against things, I never go back. I like a man who's for something.

"Like you know, I've been marshal here and there, but never had much trouble with folks. I leave their politics and religion be. Folks can think the way they want, act the way they please, even to acting the fool. All I ask is they don't make too much noise and don't interfere with other people.

"They call me a peace officer, and I try to keep the peace. If a growed-up man gets himself into a game with a crooked gambler, I don't bother them . . . if he hasn't learned up to then, he may learn, and if he doesn't learn, nothing I tell him will do him any good."

"You think Colvin was really dead?"

"Doc said so."

"Suppose he was hypnotized? Suppose he wasn't really dead at all?"

After, Brennen went to bed I saddled up and rode out of town. Circling around the mountain I rode up to where Brother Elisha used to go to pray. Brennen had left me with a thought, and Doc had been drinking a better brand of whiskey lately.

Brace had drawn money from the bank, and so had Ralston, and old Mrs. Greene had been digging out in her hen coop, and knowing about those tin cans she buried there after her husband died kind of sudden, I had an idea what she was digging up.

I made tracks. I had some communicatin' to do and not many hours to do it in.

I spent most of those hours in the

saddle. Returning to Red Horse the way I did brought me to a place where the trail forked, and one way led over behind that mountain with the burnt-off slope. When I had my horse out of sight I drew up and waited.

It was just growing gray when a rider came down the mountain trail and stopped at the forks. It was Ed Colvin.

We hadn't anything to talk about right at the moment so I just kept out of sight in the brush and then followed. He seemed like he was going to meet somebody and I had a suspicion it was Brother Elisha. And it was.

"You got it?" Ed Colvin asked.

"Of course. I told you we could fool these yokels. Now let's--"

When I stepped out of the brush I was holding a shotgun. I said, "The way of the transgressor is hard. Give me those saddlebags, Delbert."

Brother Elisha stared at me. "I fear there is some mistake," he said with dignity. "I am Brother Elisha."

"I found those cans and sacks up top of the hill. The ones where you kept your grub and the grass seed you scattered." I stepped in closer.

"You are Delbert Johnson," I

added, "and the wires over at Russian Junction say you used to deal a crooked game of faro in Mobeetie. Now give me the saddlebags."

The reverend has a new church now, and a five-room frame parsonage to replace his tiny cabin. The dead of Red Horse sleep peacefully and there is a new iron fence around the cemetery to keep them securely inside. Brennen still keeps his saloon, but he also passes the collection plate of a Sunday, and the results are far better than they used to be.

There was a lot of curiosity as to where the reverend came by the money to do the building, and the good works that followed. Privately, the reverend told Brennen and me about a pair of saddlebags he found inside the parsonage door that Sunday morning. But when anyone else asked him he had an answer ready.

"The ravens have provided," he would say, smiling gently, "as they did for Elijah."

Nobody asked any more questions.

Beau L'Amour
June 2019

ABOUT LOUIS L'AMOUR

*"I think of myself in the oral tradition—
as a troubadour, a village taleteller, the man
in the shadows of the campfire. That's the way
I'd like to be remembered—as a storyteller.
A good storyteller."*

IT IS DOUBTFUL that any author could be as at
home in the world re-created in his novels as Louis
Dearborn L'Amour. Not only could he physically fill the
boots of the rugged characters he wrote about, but he
literally "walked the land my characters walk." His personal experiences as well as his lifelong devotion to historical research combined to give Mr. L'Amour the unique
knowledge and understanding of people, events, and the
challenge of the American frontier that became the hall-
marks of his popularity.

As a boy growing up in Jamestown, North Dakota, he
absorbed all he could about his family's frontier heri-
tage, including the story of his great-grandfather who
was scalped by Sioux warriors.

Spurred by an eager curiosity and a desire to broaden
his horizons, Mr. L'Amour left home at the age of fifteen
and enjoyed a wide variety of jobs, including seaman,
lumberjack, elephant handler, skinner of dead cattle,
miner, and officer in the Transportation Corps during

World War II. He was a voracious reader and collector of books. His personal library contained 17,000 volumes.

Mr. L'Amour "wanted to write almost from the time I could talk." After developing a widespread following for the many frontier and adventure stories he wrote for fiction magazines, Mr. L'Amour published his first full-length novel, *Hondo,* in the United States in 1953. Every one of his more than 120 books is in print; there are more than 300 million copies of his books in print worldwide, making him one of the bestselling authors in modern literary history. His books have been translated into twenty languages, and more than forty-five of his novels and stories have been made into feature films and television movies.

His hardcover bestsellers include *The Lonesome Gods, The Walking Drum* (his twelfth-century historical novel), *Jubal Sackett, Last of the Breed,* and *The Haunted Mesa.* His memoir, *Education of a Wandering Man,* was a leading bestseller in 1989. Audio dramatizations and adaptations of many L'Amour stories are available from Random House Audio.

The recipient of many great honors and awards, in 1983 Mr. L'Amour became the first novelist ever to be awarded the Congressional Gold Medal by the United States Congress in honor of his life's work. In 1984 he was also awarded the Medal of Freedom by President Reagan.

Louis L'Amour died on June 10, 1988.